T0086354

While Searching for
Maaleh Ashan

While Searching for
Maaleh Ashan

Katarina Glozic

WHILE SEARCHING FOR MAALEH ASHAN

iUniverse books may be ordered through booksellers or by contacting:

iUniverse
1663 Liberty Drive
Bloomington, IN 47403
www.iuniverse.com
844-349-9409

ISBN: 978-1-6632-2041-7 (sc)
ISBN: 978-1-6632-2042-4 (e)

Print information available on the last page.

iUniverse rev. date: 06/01/2021

Dear Reader,

You are about to turn a page to a story that is loosely hinged on the facts and mostly based on dreams. It is not inspired by the experience of anyone known to the author. You are going to read about the journey that started with grieving, turned into travelling and developed into soul-searching. At moments, the narrative is heart wrenching, but it ends with the bliss of happiness.

Infringing on the memories of the people who lived many centuries ago should start with an apology. I, the author, apologize to those you are going to meet in the discourse following this personal address. Though many characters depicted in the tale have their place in the recorded history, most of their adventures and quests inside the pages of the book are the creation of imagination. They are included in the narrative to fill the gaps in knowledge of Shlomo Molcho's misfortunes. Vittoria Colonna was a poet, and a noblewoman known for her virtue and kind heart. Not a single line in the chronicles of the events testifying to Rabbi Molcho's martyrdom mentions the two being together at any social gathering.

Rabbis and communities in Israel, real, well- known, and respected, have encountered none of the characters from the story that follows. The heroes and heroines brought to life on the pages of this book are just the messengers. Any attempt to make a connection between them and the reality at any point of space and time would not add to a better understanding of the plot. It is possible that characters under different names scattered throughout the vast world over many centuries resemble living people or events. If this occurred to you while reading, blame the author's wish to make her dreams as vivid as possible.

Yours truly,
Katarina G.

PART ONE

Prayer, Meditation, or Mantra

A long time after the Second Temple was destroyed, a child was born and raised in a faraway land, south of the mists of the Pale. His childhood passed with few memories to cherish. His youth did not abound with joy. There was no great misfortune imbued by destiny upon him and his family, and he was grateful for this act of mercy by heaven. He pondered over this in his mind's eye; he tried to ward off all ill-meant spells that would damage the peaceful thread of his existence. Some would claim he needed the special mantra to succeed. The others preached about the power of prayers or meditation. The mystics recommended holy relics and amulets. Alas, according to his own judgement, all advice resembled a line drawn in the sand. Life has been a monotonous flow of events with little or no impact on the world outside the family. The eulogy that would be told at his wake could fit into three brief sentences: He was born and raised in this place. He lived and worked in this place. Eventually, he died and was buried at a local cemetery. Yes, life so far was like stale water in a glass. A life lived with little or no excitement. Gabriel Marcus grew in a cocoon of the middle-class family, in the middle-class home, partaking in middle-class leisure. Sometimes he was wondering where all stories of buried treasures and deaths enshrined in mystery came from. Grandeur and falling from grace, curses, and gnomes rushed straight from the scenery of fairy tales into the stories he heard about the family's past. Still, the landscape of his days was moderately bright, only sometimes grey, and always fitted into the well-established routine. He could not understand the controversy tagging him since the earliest age. He understood the circumstances of his living being ordinary, boring, and broken by occasional simple

1

pleasures. Therefore, he objected when told he was the last in a line of martyrs to take the duty of carrying the sceptre of truth throughout and beyond his life's time.

'The above must be a lie or a bold exaggeration of never recorded historic facts', said the cousin historian by profession to Gabriel Marcus.

'If it is a lie poorly hidden within specks of truth,' replied young Gabriel, only thirteen. 'Why am I not able to harness the tumultuous winds raging through my soul? I have been sprucing up wishful thoughts, garnishing them with borrowed ideas, painting over the reds and blacks with less exciting colours, said Gabriel quietly. Nobody heard him.

You cannot cheat your soul, Gabriel Marcus, the loud voice of your conscious and subconscious growing stronger and crying out: there is longing in you, deep, pleading to be named, yet escaping all naming games. It has the likeness of insatiable thirst, the burning glitter at the edge of the dark cloud. It makes you yearn and cleave to the ephemeral that changes into the sickly presence in the soul, persistent and incurable. Malaise. Sadness. It was, it is, it will be. You can handle it only when it takes on the shape of the people. You can bring it within the grasp of comprehensible in rare moments of clarity. Otherwise, it ravages through in the storm's manner, towering above and crushing down with no hope left in its wake.

You have the darkest of secrets, Gabriel Marcus. You do not know who you are.

A Letter from the Grave

Silence. Admire its simplicity. Stay away from confusing thoughts, empty words embedded into worn-out phrases. Take it into your heart and remember the days before they shaped us into colourless puppets with dead eyes. We stood proudly in the face of misfortune and failure. We seized every chance to light the stars and diminish the darkness. The dance of blind fate made our hearts beat with a new rhythm. We knew they denied us hope and yet did not stumble. Then, suddenly, I lost you. There was a day when I had to wake up without you and breathe in loneliness. The moment of understanding, the finality of the parting. The time to accept the unacceptable. Your eyes changed from sapphire blue to the dull glitter of glass. I could not remember your smile. You turned into a grim presence in the back of my mind. The puppet with dead eyes. You faded and became nothing but a shadow.

He looked at the pages spread on the table. This was one of many times that he went over the words trying to decode emotions that inspired and pushed the hand that wrote them. Was this a literary exercise or a cry of the soul fighting the despair? The instinct told him he had been on the wrong track. He was looking for a way to decode the message. Was there one? Even if it was there, was his purpose to understand it? The poems Anna wrote were about darkness and desolation. They questioned the integrity of the author. They differed from anything he knew about her. When he read them the first time, it felt like a strike of a lightning. She was never the one to wallow in sadness; she was a grit in the face of a challenge. The handwriting was hers, yet the verses were more the literary exercise than a confession, soliloquy detached from the original character of a poet, delivered from a great distance, remote in time and space. He entered this into the journal as the note about the sadness that was not Anna's yet killed her somehow. The piece of poetry was not in any way inspired by him. He was not that long-lost love that made her sad, that breathed the air of solitude into her words and her heart. During the four years they spent together, he never sensed nor inspired anything that could have transpired into dead-eyed puppets. He loved her. They had a relationship devoid of major conflicts and misunderstandings. Yet, this ominous note was in the box at the bottom of her closet labelled 'in case of sudden parting' and his name inscribed underneath. It took many searches through the content to wear off guilt and remorse. He could not understand. The lack of understanding did not make him innocent. Sometimes, we are blind to the pains and sorrows of others, even when they are close. Unless they open their mouth and articulate what hurts them, the spells of sadness may go unnoticed, unheard, and turn into despair, and despair into the state of mind that slowly erodes any hope for repair. These thoughts haunted him for days after he went through the content of the box she left behind–the message from beyond the grave that was not for him, yet his to understand.

Memories of Salonica

In a flash of memory, he saw the face of a young woman in his mind. Her name was Adah, and he stayed with her family during his first time in the city. They were all sitting together after the evening meal, involved in chatting and laughs. He might have glanced at her too long or spoke in a voice too endearing - and her smile, shy at first, turned into a strange outburst of passion at night. She did not seem interested in him during the dinner and conversation that went on in her father's elegant living room. Still, some hours later, she quickly slipped out of her night-gown, untied the hair that smelled of lavender and summer night and tried to lie next to him.

The letter from Professor Vasiliadis came out of the blue. It informed him briefly of the research it involved him in, accompanied by copies of letters and documents, and the invitation to join him in Salonica for a few days. He also asked about any other relevant records of family history that Gabriel could bring along in return for paid travel expenses. Winter was waning and spring must have been already in full power in the south. He booked the flight and packed. Three weeks after the letter, he was skipping the stairs of a long and steep stairway on the way to his destination and destiny.

How It Came to Be

At the opening of the fifteenth century, the change in political powers ended with the expulsion from Spain and Portugal. Khmelnitsky massacres performed with cruelty difficult to fathom resulted in the demise of over a hundred thousand Jews, and three times as many displaced people. Forced conversions, persecution, and lack of proper leadership in the chaos of fleeing from imminent danger opened the door to several messianic candidates over a few decades of the sixteenth and early seventeenth century. Great suffering often seeks to be eased by illusions, resulting in social unrest and revolutions. History of suffering of Jews recorded a few temporary, yet passionate obsession with Messianic movements. It is difficult to judge people for trying to find hope in a hopeless world. I should think no one evil for trying to break free from the mortal coil repeatedly imposed on one group of human beings, seeking their extinction. None of the people that embarked on a journey of turning despair into hope and moved thousands with the power of faith did this for vain reasons. Were these people misguided? Definitely. Were some of them mentally ill? We can only guess, but most probably, they were. Were they necessary and useful to the communities during the most troublesome times they were going through? From the perspective of the Pogroms of the late nineteenth, and the Holocaust in the twentieth century; the count of the dead that hit millions, the above lot of the false messiahs were just the messengers of the new era. Their existence was the gestation period preceding the spiritual revolution of Hasidism and the whole new understanding of Jewish theology, different way of living, altered perception of reality. It made the ideal of consistent worship and growing from the ashes of destruction real and attainable. At the end of the beginning of the road, political communities of the world had to welcome the new, independent state of Israel. Thus, it turns out that David Reubeni, Shlomo Molcho, Shabbatai Tzvi, Jacob Frank, though cursed more than lauded while alive and dead, were drinking from the same well as Rabbi Luria, Joseph Caro, and Baal Shem Tov. They were the men of extreme measures that fitted extreme times they lived in. It was the world that threatened the physical and spiritual existence of Jewish communities that pushed them into the roles they had taken. False messiahs were children of great pain, fear, and despair.

David Reubeni attempted to inspire the war of all Christendom against Islam, which he paid with his life. Christian rulers congregating around Rome did not understand the value of freeing their Byzantine brothers from the Muslim oppressors. They also would not have any respect for the Jewish rule and faith in the Holy Land. To the less passionate eye, the liberation of non-kosher Christians would only open grounds for schism and dogmatic discord and result in a diminished power of the Pope, or even dispersing of power to places other than Rome.

Jewish 'Messiahs' were all about fulfilling their mission as God's servants. Even when they were dangerously deviant, and their actions were detached from reason they were gifted with powerful faith. Regardless of the fact that the spiritual authorities considered their ways unacceptable; their attempt to elevate all creation through unusual means devoid of sanity contributed to better understanding of the circumstances and times leading to the ultimate redemption.

At that point in history, their non-Jewish counterparts governing over Jews in various parts of Europe were cleaving to political power and material wealth, a larger number of serfs and other resources under the firm control of the church. Their faith seldom lifted itself from the temptations of the flesh, even when they pledged the earthly pleasures on the altar of celibacy, fasting and lengthy prayers. The irony of the construct must have pushed them toward ultimate hypocrisy: the most pious of Christians were praying to the dead Jew after all; That could not have been ignored even by moderately intelligent followers of the faith. The object of worship in Christianity was founded on the concept of transcendental monotheism of Jewish faith. Understanding of monotheism was often impossible to the souls immersed in pagan practices, rituals, and beliefs few centuries before. Human mind that attached its belief to tangible objects of worship was up for a challenge: the faith in omnipotent, omnipresent deity that is invisible, transcendental, and immanent source of everything. The new milestone.

Shlomo Molcho and David Reubeni were two in a line of messianic candidates that sparked hope in the chaos of expulsions from Spain and Portugal. The former was born into the family of new Christians and named Diogo Pires. Renamed after the conversion, or rather the return from conversion, Shlomo was a most passionate believer. He almost bled to death after performing circumcision on himself as an adult. At the beginning of his spiritual journey, inspired by the meeting with lustrous adventurer David Reubeni, he wanted to learn about Judaism and follow his teacher on many Mediterranean adventures. Alas, he was rejected unless circumcised and the famed event of self-mutilation took place and was publicized. This resulted in the order for the expulsion from Portugal for both the teacher and the disciple. Besides, David Reubeni was accused of inspiring deflection among Portuguese

Marranos. King John III of Portugal would have had him incarcerated; the teacher and his disciple had to move and resume their work in Italy. At some point, they separated, and Solomon Molcho was on his own until the joint meeting with the 'Holy Emperor of Rome'. In the end, they shared the same destiny by the orders of that Charles V Regensburg. They were to be questioned and tried by the Inquisition in Mantua. David Reubeni was poisoned in the dungeons of the Spanish inquisition or burned at the stake. Shlomo Molcho was burned at the stake in Mantua, on the 5th of Tevet in the year 1532.

During the last decade of his brief life as a rebel and a Rabbi, Shlomo Molcho travelled from Portugal to Italy, Turkey, and Israel. On his way to the Holy Land, he stayed in Salonica. He was the contemporary of Joseph Caro and respected as a gifted student of the famous cabbalist Rabbi Joseph Tzaitzak. His writings about his dreams and cabbalistic concepts of the Torah, if authentic and uncensored, can be found in the Kitvei Shlomo Molcho. He also published Derashot, the exegesis on the Bible, based mostly on the Talmud and Midrash in 1529. During his brief life as a Jew, he never referred to himself as a Messiah but spoke about the times that would usher one. Those claiming the opposite are guilty of slander. He died as a martyr at thirty-two. Much later, Rabbi Chaim Vital would connect his name to a lot of the ill-fated scholars of mysticism who experimented with the practical kabbalah.

With this 'accusation' Rabbi Vital added the lore of mysticism to Rabbi Molcho's tireless struggle to bring light to those suffering in the darkness. The rhetoric about kabbalah was an attempt to find the convoluted explanation for his martyrdom and inspire others to set on a path of repairing the world. There were many who wanted to right the wrong. Shlomo Molcho was a child of the marranos who suffered the conversion but never undertook the conversion in their heart. He chose the road less travelled to fix the damage done to the communities in Spain and Portugal. This battle fought by the few often ended with martyrdom. The fight against the decrees issued by the Inquisition and Christian kings, the protectors of the power of Rome, was equal to hitting the head against the wall. Some chose the noble way to die and did not denounce their faith. They did not pay lip service to the murderers. The others did. There was little to choose from; though it was difficult to accept the contradictory state of affairs, the spiritual death of conversion to Christianity gave more hope for the spiritual resurrection. Shlomo Molcho was born and baptised as Diogo Pires. He was the second generation of the swine. Yet he passionately embraced the faith of his ancestors. Those who did not denounce Jewish religion either died or were exiled.

Gabriel Marcus was the only known descendant of Rabbi Molcho. While they were reflecting upon this, his mother packed their family photographs and memories, connecting her to the people that lived decades and centuries ago. Everything Professor Vasiliadis could find useful for his work was packed in the black leather suitcase laid on the floor. Gabriel's mother was a brisk, tiny woman who moved around with quick motions resembling the squirrel. She was always smiling. With the spark of humorous mischief in sapphire blue eyes, Adele Marcus told her son the tragic story of his great-great-great-grandfather and those after him in a low voice and whisper. Whenever she was about to mention her family history, she would look around, lean forward, and talk with obvious fear that unwanted ears might hear what she had to say. Gabriel found her fears irritating, but reasonable. Most of their relatives died in the Holocaust. They were not spared in wars and pogroms of earlier times, too. This suffering was received with docile patience by those who learned about the limitations of their options in this world.

Elegy

'When we parted, my beloved, the shine of luminaries lost their beauty and skies shaded. Since we parted, I have been wandering from place to place, inconsolable and without peace. My robes are covered in ashes, my eyes weary of tears. My home has been laying desolate, its hearth dark and cold. The flowers wilted at the doorstep and roses were overtaken by thorns. I have been searching for any trace of your presence in forty-two places and inquired in six more - grim silence was given to me as an answer. Where have you gone, my beloved, why have you been silent? Neither lamentations nor devoted prayers brought you back. Speak to me, my beloved, make this exile cease, turn bitter cry into joyous singing. Return light to our dwelling place, to the lodging of our love, my beloved. Long wanderings made me desolate, and my body is weakened from long-suffering. Will I ever be in your presence again, and my heart consoled and elevated?'

The note was yellow and crumbling at the edges. Fine paper threads have almost disintegrated into powder in Gabriel's hands. He laid it on the table to read instead of holding it. Ink faded over time, and words were hard to make out. Gabriel paused after each word and held his breath with fear that something may cause the letters to dissolve and disappear into thin air. He also tried to imagine the circumstances that inspired the verses that cried to heaven to open and end long wandering. They were written by his grandfather in his youth while he still lived his life in relative safety. They were created a long time before he perished in the Shoah with other twenty-three members of his family. Gabriel's mother said that his grandfather was a pious man, hardworking, quiet, and kind. She did not remember him and had to scrape a few images from her earliest childhood to look for any memories of his existence. This was not a simple job, and she would be overwhelmed with sorrow whenever she attempted to do so. Her father was not a Rabbi, yet he spent many hours learning and praying.

After the war broke out and raged through Greece, he closed his business and tried but failed to move to Palestine. The hopeless drifting began. It was difficult to keep the family of five in hiding. It was difficult to move three young children from one village to another, travel only on the darkest of nights, deprived of light of the moon on the road. The nights with darkness thick as wool were the only safe time for travelling but could not save him, his wife, and two of their children. Only the youngest, Adele, survived. She was less than a year old and gladly taken by the family of farmers who offered them shelter for a few weeks. As she could not talk, it was easy to mix her with the farmer's children. She was just another little girl in a household. That is how it came to be that Adele was the only survivor, while others perished in the death camps. She was told her actual name and the fate of her family, as soon as age would allow her to understand what had become of her mother, father, and siblings. Adele was too young to comprehend why she had to hide, or why it was dangerous to be a Jew. It killed her family–that is what she could make out at an early stage in life. It was deadlier than all known diseases, afflictions, and ailments together. Worse than famines and other natural disasters. It was impossible to understand, but it had to be accepted as the only truth offered. Adele accepted her destiny and carried on living in a world that hated and killed people just because they were Jews.

After the war ended, the family connected Adele to the relatives who survived. They contacted the centre for the displaced people; the messages were exchanged, and the beautiful blue-eyed girl had set on another journey into the unknown.

Gabriel was thinking about the family of farmers who risked their lives to hide his mother, her siblings, and parents when Adah came into his bedroom and undressed. She was watching him with a silent grin, expectant of passionate approval, verbal response, a kiss. She got nothing of the above. Gabriel rested his head on the pillow, eyes shut in the manner of a dog that went through obedience school and uttered in a soft voice:

'You should not be doing this. I would not abuse your father's hospitality and put our work at risk because of your whims. Put your nightgown on and go back to your room. No, I have nothing against you or your body. You are beautiful. Please, go. Goodnight.' Gabriel said calmly.

And just like that, as he completed the last sentence, he turned his face to the wall and waited for the girl to leave. He was not tempted to act differently. He was not enticed by her youth, beauty and brazenness. Only six months before, somebody that made all the difference in his life left for good. He could still remember the smell of her skin on his hands, the soft line of her neck, the belly that cleaved to his heaps while they moved to each other to become one. People should not be allowed to die without giving those they leave behind enough time to prepare; the deceased is not the only one in need of a reasonable amount of time to understand and accept the passage from life to the realm of death. It took him, the lover of the young woman, a long time to internalise the chain of events that took place on the fated day. It was Tuesday morning. She stepped outside to run some errands and never came back. She never said goodbye or anything like. There was no warning, no anticipation of the inevitable.

His Anna was snatched out of his arms by cruel destiny, and he was left alone to face the desperate call from her parents, broken body covered in blood, police report of the accident, news in the local paper, obituaries in the national paper, funeral he did not attend, empty universe reverberating the images, sounds, smells that are no more, or will ever be again. He grew envious of young, beautiful girls walking in the streets. The thought that went through his head was inconsolable; they live, walk, laugh, legs propped on high heels, lips lined with lipstick, skin bathed in fragrance - and his Anna was no more. Beautiful, young, kind Anna was turned into a bundle of blood and broken bones and buried. Never to laugh, make love, sing, and call him the names known only to two of them.

Adah's exhibitionism did not make any impression on him. It was a painful recall of the moments of intimacy shared with his lost love. He waited until the girl got dressed and left his room. Then, he jumped out of the bed and spent the rest of the night in the armchair facing the window. The round fullness of the moon hanging from the sky carried him off to sleep. In the morning, he moved into a small hotel in the neighbourhood.

Close to Meron

We do not know the name of Tsfat at the time of the Temple. The earliest evidence of the physical existence of the town dates from Cairo genizah. It is mentioned as the sanctuary for the priestly families that fled Jerusalem before the Roman army. During the middle ages, it has grown to become the home of modern-day Jewish mysticism and poetry that is part of the liturgy throughout the Jewish world. Tsfat is a rose between the hills, a nest of an eagle, a resting place of beautiful names. It is often called a cradle for the Messiah. The stories about the town and its history lighten the heart and bring words of praise to lips. Many stories can be told about this town in Northern Galilee from the times of the destruction of the Temple until modern days.

Rabbi Abohav, Rabbi Cordovero, Rabbi Luria, Joseph Caro, Shlomo Alkabetz, and dozens of others rest in the Old Cemetery. Tsfat is a quiet place - filled with whispers of prayers that made it a symbol of hope. Its future was envisioned in the holy writings. It is a place destined to be a birthplace of the redeemer; It is said that the King will be born here on the darkest date of the year. The dawn will be announced in the midnight prayers. The ultimate redemption will begin on the date of the destruction of many centuries before.

This is where Shlomo Molcho arrived in the spring of 1531. He travelled through Italy, Turkey and preached at the gates of Jerusalem before taking up on the steep stairways, and through narrow town streets. Rabbi Taitazak gave him the letter for his relative, a small-scale merchant who traded wool and wine throughout Galilee. The man mostly stayed in Tsfat. The roads and ports were not safe, and he could not afford armed guards on his ventures. As he was telling Rabbi Molcho, the times were dreadful, and he hardly managed. This was not entirely true. The times were filled with uncertainty, perils, and fear, but the short and stout man was the only son of a wealthy father who secured most of his wealth from Spain. A cousin to Rabbi Taitazak, full of respect for the scholar, he took the advice of his relative seriously and removed his gold from Spain many years before the decree issued by Ferdinand and Isabella. He never spoke much of it; however, it was the wealth big enough to support most of the immediate and extended family and ensure their survival in Turkey and the Land. Humble, he lived modestly by trading wool and wine. The business was taken over by his eldest son, who offered hospitality to Solomon Molcho at the request of his famous relative.

Even in this epoch, the town was the labyrinth of stairs and tall fences guarding from views of the occasional passer-by. Rabbi Molcho became the friend of Moses Alkabetz. Both fled the persecution of Inquisition and wandered about the Mediterranean before settling in Tsfat. Now they spent hours learning together. Molcho came to town from Salonica; he learned the kabbalah of the squares with Rabbi Taitazak, the halachic authority respected from the shores of Salonica to Damascus and Jerusalem. He was famous for the knowledge of the squares and the amulets. At the time of Molcho's travels the multitude of Jewish people believed in amulets, both as powerful shields held in protection, and a weapon against foes. The teacher taught Molcho about the secret inscriptions and divine names corresponding to the six directions, as they are explained in the Bahir. Even though these were studied only in connection with the mysteries of creation, many were tempted to use them for the revenge on their foes.

It is not known how much young scholar learned from a cabbalist. The knowledge that he gained is thought responsible for his premature death. He has summoned the angels of the sixth chamber to help him glance at the future. He has seen what was hidden. He made use of the name which is known as the Crown (that being the secret divine name that should not be pronounced). It is believed and taught that whoever makes use of the Crown loses his place in this and the world to come. This was written by Rabbi Chaim Vital, the righteous, who did not engage in using practical cabbalah. The writings of Rabbi Vital are the only record of the teachings and adventures of Rabbi Luria, and the only mention of the erroneous dealings with the celestial powers of Shlomo Molcho. The exact words of Rabbi Vital on the matter are:

'Husks attach themselves to the individual who attempts to gain enlightenment through the Practical Kabbalah. We also have a tradition that such an individual will be punished in this world and in the world to come Then he goes on with listing the names of those who succumbed to the temptation and cursing them, respectively.'

The Other Side

The morning was unfolding over the pond. Skies were bright on the eastern horizon, the water full of whispers and gurgles, sloshing and cracking deep under the ice. The colours were beautiful, yet bitterly cold air would bite mercilessly into the skin if exposed. The group of shivering bodies emerged from the forest and stumbled into the clearing. They were followed by the guards and their dogs. Ill-dressed, emaciated silhouettes moved through the snow, glided down the slippery paths while trying to keep a safe distance from the barking dogs. They hardly had any strength to balance themselves during this long, aimless stroll. One guard yelled the command, and everybody stood still. The man stumbled; a group quickly made room and propped him up. Weakness was punished with a bullet at the back of the head, on the spot. A miserable group of used to be human beings gently supported the one that could not stand on ice-clad soil. The soles of his shoes were paper thin, and rags wrapped around feet hardly offered any protection against the cold. The man was burning with fever and delirious. He stumbled while mumbling, voice getting louder with every word: 'Adele! Adele! Adele!' The cries coming from the skeleton burning with fever were too loud, and the guards were now looking in man's direction.

The body next to him punched him slightly, then leaned over and stuck a ball of fabric into his mouth; He spoke Yiddish -short but clear warnings of what might come if he continued to scream or even whisper. Those with the dogs were coming closer, and they had no patience or understanding for moaning, stumbling, feverish prisoners. If they completed the digging, they would be taken back, or they would be shot to death and somebody else would be brought to dig the graves. It was as simple as that, and their only goal was to complete the task and drag themselves back into the barracks before it got colder again. The man did not seem to respond to what was told. He was staring beyond the faces of the inmates, dogs, and guards—eyes fixated into the mist rising above the bare trees, golden and glittery in the morning sun. 'Adele' he shouted, and then again - with this name on his lips, he broke free of the group and ran back towards the forest.

The rest of the party will remember that he had his arms wide open as if to fly, head turned to the sky and the sun. For a moment, it seemed he was floating above the frozen soil, and everybody expected and hoped he would fly away. But he had not. After the first bullet, he fell to the ground in the manner of a broken rag doll, and the second fired bullet was a waste. Uriel was already gone, his eyes and a smile full of the blue sky and the rising sun. The mist lingered at the edge of the forest, took a shape of a beautiful woman, golden and warm - then faded and turned into a grey drizzle over the muddy puddles. In deadly silence, the inmates pushed the shovels into the frozen ground with no visible acknowledgement of the event.

Adele opened dented, scratched suitcase with squeaky locks and stained lining that was the only connection to her parents, brother, and sister. She had no memories of them. When her family was taken to a death camp, Adele was ten months old. Raised in the household of Greek farmers, she learned about her biological parents at five, after the war ended, when it was safe to call her by her true name and mentioning Jews would get nobody imprisoned and murdered. The suitcase was given to her before she left for Salonica and from there further to the north to a new home offered by the relatives of her mother that escaped calamities of war. They had never met Adele or her family before, neither did they know what had become of them. The letter sent from the centre for the displaced people reached them shortly after the war. There were few Jews left in Northern Greece. Adele was registered at the centre in Salonica and while there was nobody that claimed her, a good Samaritan found the relatives living as far as Belgrade, in the former Kingdom of Yugoslavia, and let them know she had survived the war and details of her whereabouts. A few months after the letter was dispatched, Uncle Shmuli and Aunt Estelle arrived at the farm of Adele's adoptive parents, and the journey into the uncertainty began. She became Adela, Lela, or simply sweetheart. Shmu–as she called her uncle while still at the stage of learning a new language and Ella, were the first real blessing in her life. They made her feel less alone, less deprived of safe, carefree, and joyous childhood that she could not have before. Until arrival at their home, all she knew was fear, sorrow, and deprivation. After a few weeks, she started laughing at jokes for the first time since birth, enjoyed listening to the stories at bedtime and soon engaged in playing with the children from the neighbourhood. Shmu and Ella cooked her favourite dishes, baked cookies shaped like stars with raspberry jam in the centre, and made clothes for her dolls out of crinkled paper and shiny ribbons. They took her to the riverbank and marketplace on Sunday. As she grew older, they started talking about her education and future vocation. They spoke to her about Israel. Her aunt and uncle did not have children of their own, have never had them, and were planning to move to the newly announced state of Israel before their health and strength left them. It was not an easy undertaking and had to be approached with caution and planning. They did not pressure Adele to move with them but hoped that she would visit; possibly fall in love with the land and stay. These good people, like many other surviving European Jews, were tired of hatred, persecution and constant danger looming over the communities throughout the old continent. The hostility of the local population and vast areas with little vegetation were more welcoming landscape than the cities ravaged by war, food rationing and emerging communist regimes that promised nothing good to Jews either. Little trust was left in Jewish communities throughout Europe, and most of it perished in the crematoria of Auschwitz. Barren rocks of Judean desert, mosquitos, and humidity of the coastal plains with nothing on them were surmountable difficulties. Hills of ashes of nameless human beings on the grounds of the concentration camps were the wall separating them from the countries they considered their home. From the moment it came to be, it would always be present. Till the End of Time. Even out of use, empty and cold, the crematoria of Auschwitz were a memory of destruction. Everyone will remember trains that were taking people to the end of all journeys and hopes. People cannot survive without hope. Therefore, they had to pack and leave Europe for the land that was overflowing with hope and little of anything else. The stories of miracles made possible by the Zionists were re-told by surviving members of the communities everywhere, with glitter in the eyes and joyous souls.

Photographs, letters, few journals, business agreements that belonged to her father made most of the content of the suitcase that was given to Adele on the day when Uncle Shmuli came to pick her up. The only part of this lot that could interest anybody other than the family member or a passionate historian trying to save the chronicles and adventures of the family from oblivion were ten small pieces of parchments with different content inscribed. Images of various symbols and letters written in black covered every inch of their surface. On top of these, pressed and disfigured - a rag doll. It was not known whether it belonged to Adele or her sister; she had no recollection of ever playing with it. Doll's hair was made of fine golden colour threads, the dress embroidered and laced all over; still exquisitely beautiful despite all the years of use, and a long time pressed in a suitcase. Face took the worst beating - one eye was missing, and the nose was pushed into the flannel chick. The precious toy that was handed to a five-year-old girl was received with solemn silence and subdued wondering; she took the doll with both hands and held it with caution to prevent any potential damage her grip may cause. This would repeat many years later, when Adele was packing Gabriel's suitcase for his trip to Salonica. While she pondered over the photographs, letters, and documents that Professor Vasiliadis asked for, she took the doll out again and held it as a little girl. She never played with it. It was the only remaining evidence of the existence of other children in the family - she knew it was not hers, and it was to be kept until her sister, or her mother, came to claim it. There was another reason that made this toy almost holy to a five-year-old girl. When she had it for the first time, little fingers went over the dress and felt something hard inside. She pressed in and took out the little box made of silver hidden inside the belly of the doll. The box was tucked into the soft filling of the tummy, easy to grab, and she simply ripped it out of the doll's innards' tearing the fragile fabric and clotted cotton 'flesh'. The box was oval and light, with etched shapes all over the lid. They were Hebrew letters: Mem-kaf-bet-yud - four Hebrew letters in the middle of the flag on a pole carried by the lion. She shook the box - it was empty. Adele pushed it back into the cotton wool of the doll's stuffing and told nobody about it. It was her big secret. Something she would take out and hold when she was sad, ill, or simply felt lost in this world.

The Journey

Gabriel occupied a small room at Vourla, modestly priced hotel close to the pier. Salonica summer was in full swing. He turned forty a few days before and could not take the hustle and bustle of the big cities anymore. Today, he has been suffering from headache, melancholy, and bad memories. Last night, he spent hours planning out the rest of his trip. Salonica was only a stopover on his route to Israel. He did not have any set plans, neither scheduled meetings with those waiting for him in Tel Aviv and Jerusalem. The names of these places were contours at the back of his mind, not the reality. They were destinations at various stages of his itinerary. Vaguely, he knew he must make more tangible plans for the next part of the journey. He tried to push himself into a more enthusiastic feeling for the adventure of moving from one of the Mediterranean towns to another. Blazing heat followed him anywhere he went and made the journey ultimately exhausting. From the onset of this adventure, he resisted taking advice from anyone; not a wise decision; it took revenge on his well-being.

As he did not share plans and insisted on privacy, he had to do everything on his own, which backfired and left him to cope with issues related to scheduling, booking, and searching besides packing and unpacking, correspondence related to his stay in different places and simple map navigation wherever he went. While this appeared manageable and affordable at the planning stage of the journey, he felt already exhausted at the first stop, Salonica. He tried but failed to make his undertaking enjoyable, not even close to pleasure. He had an old, unresolved problem with his sleep, which only got worse over time and deteriorated during the trip. On most nights he got little sleep, and today he lived in the shadow of last night's nightmare. He would describe his dreams as nightmares only by the impact they had on him the following day. All his dreams were nightmares. They were heavy with sorrow, longing, and despair. This one had left him shaking with inexplicable fear, too. Sometimes after three, Gabriel jumped out of his bed, delirious and soaked in sweat. For a few moments, he could not remember what startled him; the sweat bids were rolling down the forehead, his heart was racing, and mouth turned coarse and dry. Whatever drenched his body in terror seemed to have moved from the realm of dreams to his room. The evil presence stretched over the walls and floor. His mind was frantically trying to recover the images and hints of whatever came over while he was asleep. He tried to catch the meaning behind fear and was thinking of the incident that emerged as a reason for this quest. When the heartbeat returned to normal, and he swallowed a few sips of water, it was easier to go over the emerging cluster of images. The panic attack gave way to the effort to preserve everything he had seen; the attempt to recall the smallest detail with any significance.

Gabriel even grabbed the pen and wrote that he saw himself (feeling detached and standing like a ghost beside his physical body) walking through the streets of a town at the seacoast; He had the memory of three ships anchored at the port, ready to embark on a long journey. Walking through the narrow streets turned into an adventure. The place seemed familiar, yet he knew he had never visited before. He was eagerly trying to find a way around and searched for the names of the streets or anything on the buildings that would give him direction. The street signs and any inscriptions he saw were in a language he did not recognise. Somehow, he knew that long ago, he could understand and read in that language. Unfortunately, that had been many years before the dream. He had lost the memory of it all. Continuously, at the back of his mind, he had been trying to think of a plan. He had to find out a way to get to the port with the anchored ships. The people he tried to ask for help did not respond to questions and passed by without a glance in his direction. All his strength was employed in the attempt to find a way through the knot of the lanes and stairways of the strange town. Yet, his efforts would end in aimless drifting from one place to another. There was nobody to help, and he knew he might never reach the ships in time. They were about to pull their anchors and set on a journey across the sea. Even worse than not being able to find a way in the labyrinth of streets and stairways, he did not know which ship he would board and for what purpose. He was drifting from one alley to the next, stumbling and falling, all alone.

In this desperate need for guidance, he walked into an arched passage that was leading to a house. The room he walked into had nothing but a bench and a table in it. They were made of beautiful white marble; the same style and size frequently commissioned for chapels of the gentry at the cemeteries across Spain or Italy. The air in the room was stale but cooling and felt good after his long walk through the cobweb of streets and allies. As he was taking a seat, exhausted from wandering around the town, his instincts warned him he was not alone. Somebody was watching from the shadows of drapes in the dark corner and though he could not make out the features of the person, he felt the presence, the one that startled him and dangled above his bed in Vourla until his mind was fully alert. It was a woman that he had seen in the dream, and she left her shelter of the drapes and quietly walked towards him. While she was getting closer, her eyes were locked on Gabriel, but at a distance of an arm's length, he realised she did not have eyes. The face of apparition did not bear any emotions, and he was uncertain whether he saw her or simply felt her presence within. A moment later she was standing close; shadows of the room were hiding her; she did not emerge from the darkness. Empty eye sockets, sealed lips, dark hair curling around the soft line of the forehead to the chin. He was on his feet again and felt with shaking fingers across the walls, searching for the doors to run through. All along, he was stricken with weakness and could not move fast, nor speak. Finally, with great effort, he articulated some words. His voice echoed in the empty chapel:

'I need to find the ship to board today. There are three of them leaving soon, ready and set, and I do not know which one to board.'

'What do you expect to find at the end of your journey, Gabriel?' the ghost responded.

Though every limb of the body was shaking with fear, his voice sounded calm and polite.

'Neither my destination nor the purpose of the journey was revealed to me.'

He could see her lips emerging from the darkness of the room as she moved closer.

'Sometimes we discover the purpose while on the journey. Sometimes we are given the signs along the way. Were you given the signs, Gabriel?

He saw himself as a child, dressed in festive clothing with pomade in his hair. This ten-year-old Gabriel was staring in the apparition's direction and said in the voice of a child:

'I was told not to replace the signs for signs. I am quite lost now. Lost in the memories of others, the quests that are not mine, strange dreams that leave me desolate.'

'You have taken the road less travelled and traded light of this world for the knowledge of the other one,' echoed the ghost.

'I just wanted to know which of the three ships would take me to my destination. I do not want to be caught in the dreams of other people. This is not my dream.'

Ten-year the old boy has had enough and wanted to be rid of the wandering and talking to the dead.

'This is not my dream.'

He screamed those words out, but did not wake up. The woman left her previous spot and glided swiftly towards the side doors that he made out only when she disappeared behind them. The door was sealed; his crying and yelling changed nothing. He was left alone in the cemetery–which became obvious as the dream unfolded. While trying to find his way back to the street, he saw another person near the gate. It turned that was a caretaker and Gabriel inquired about the woman he had just met. The response did not surprise him. The caretaker explained:

'There was no woman in the cemetery at the time you mentioned, sir. I have been here all morning and no one except you went through the gates. Most of the town people are at the docks because the ships are leaving today. They are all leaving for the colonies.'

He was trying to find out more from the caretaker, but he expired too and could be seen nowhere. Gabriel went back to the chapel in the hope to meet the mysterious apparition and shouted a few times, trying to conjure her again. The stone of the grave did not echo his voice, neither had moved the air in the corners of the room. He leaned his head on the table and drifted to sleep again. When he woke up, he noticed the oval silver box next to the bed. He could not remember when he took it out of the suitcase the night before. It was a small snuffbox with Hebrew letters on the bottom and a lion holding a banner on the lid.

The Rose

Little is left of Safed Rabbi Molcho conquered with his piety and passion. In two tragic earthquakes, most of the town's valuable monuments from the glorious days of the city were lost. Ari's synagogue, as well as the houses of those who witnessed the events of Rabbi Molcho's life, turned into dust. There was a smile in his eyes and sweet words of hope and redemption on his lips for everyone willing to listen. The place was small; the streets curved and narrowed; it was easy to pace the entire town a few times in a day. He learned and helped the cousin of his teacher. He frequented the synagogue every day. That was the same place Rabbi Luria would choose for daily prayers a few decades later. When he was not in the study house, people would meet him on the pathways around the city and not once, but many times he visited the grave of Simeon Bar Yohai. Those visits became a routine shortly after the arrival; he would disappear for a few days and would come back with the expression on the face that stems from understanding the sole purpose of one's existence. What he accepted was his destiny. The thought of it slowly cut a deep line between the eyebrows. He never spoke about his visits to Meron, and when asked, he would respond with silence or simply change the conversation. One trip to Meron did not take a long time, and he returned with the bride. When he was talking about her to the community in Tsfat, his eyes lit with the light within. A broad smile showed the line of beautiful teeth. Young Rabbi was happy, it seemed, for the first time in his life, happy and willing to share his happiness with the entire world.

The girl was not a beauty, and nothing in her appearance would attract attention at first sight. She was almost a child, slender and of fine stature, with features hidden under a scarf, whips of thick hair that pushed its way out with each move of the head. Her skin was fair, eyes blue. She moved around light as a morning cloud. Vered Zemora was a daughter of a pauper, one of those who travelled across the Mediterranean with little to begin with and reached the Holy Land completely broke and broken. He was a widower with a young child and empty pockets. He did not have any relatives to address for help on arrival, support their well-being later; Many years passed. His daughter has grown and reached the age when she should be married off. Her father was an elderly man, and his health deteriorated soon after they arrived in Holy Land. The father and the daughter lived in a crumbling one-room home close to Meron. The shack was in a decrepit condition even before they moved in. The man, involved in the spice trade previously, did not have any money to establish his business at the destination and could not offer any dowry for his daughter. Even though the girl was bright and healthy and the right age for betrothal, very few people had seen her; Rabbi Molcho met her while she was harvesting the herbs near her home. He visited on each trip to Meron and brought them whatever they needed to keep their bodies nourished and covered. After a few months, he asked for permission to marry Vered Zemora. The only dowry that was offered to the groom was the list of spices and herbs that her father compiled over the years. These were not only the list of ingredients; detailed instructions included the recommended harvest times, parts of the plants to be used to enrich the taste of various dishes or beverages. The recipes varied from cooking to compounding the remedies used to ease pain from arthritis, toothache, or headache, clean the worms from the intestines or even chase away the bad dreams. Shlomo Molcho wrote to Rabbi Taitazak about the heirloom of his newly wedded bride. He praised the work of his father-in-law and mentioned pages containing all kinds of herbs and spices that were included in the Ketoret. He mentioned in the letter:

'The most important list I found contains the names and properties of the ingredients used for Ketoret. The mixture burnt as the incense offering in the Temple has always been a secret of the trade. I have never seen so many species available to the priestly families for incense preparation.'

Angels

'The guardians at the door of the Sixth Chamber act as if they are casting millions of waves of water at the individual. However, there is not even a single drop. If the individual says: What is the purpose of this water? They pursue him and say: You, miserable creature! You are probably a descendant of those who kissed the Golden Calf! You are not worthy of seeing the King and His Throne. Then, they cast millions of steel axes at him.'

Jacob Mantino ben Samuel's body was discovered in the house's cellar he recently leased in Damascus. It was decomposing for two days before the servants found it. The examination of the remains of the deceased concluded he had died of an unknown cause. Nothing further was ordered. The mystery of his death started with the confusion regarding his whereabouts. One evening Don Mantino did not show up for his dinner at the scheduled time. The servants looked around the house. It was not usual for him to be late at the table, nor forget about his glass of raki before the meal. He had no business at that hour at the neighbour's place, yet the kitchen help was sent across the street to ask about his master's whereabouts. Nobody checked the back of the wine cellar. The master of the house did not have any business there. It was the duty of the servants to fill decanters. Nobody saw him going down the steep stairway to the part of the house that smelled of mould locked in the rotting wood and acidic fumes coming from fermenting grape juice. After the search, it was assumed he had left on some urgent, secret matter. When he had not returned by midnight, the incident was reported to the authorities He might have been kidnapped by the robbers and everyone waited for the ransom to be demanded through a messenger. Others feared Don Mantino had fallen sick or had been attacked and left to die in some deserted part of the town. His friend and business partner, Bartelemi Marcello, sent the guards all over the city to learn of his fate. Finally, two days later, a maid descended to fill the decanters with wine for the growing number of people visiting the house. She smelled something strange amidst wine vapours and took the lamp to the back of the long row of barrels. Her frightened screaming led the search party to the dark corner of the room where they found Don Mantino resting on his stomach, with face pushed into the floor as if he had fallen from a height. It did not appear he had died after rolling down the stairs. Detailed and careful examination of the body could not determine the cause of death. There were no marks to point at an accident or an attack. There were no footprints or any trace of an altercation. There was not a single item from the house reported as missing. Don Mantino carried little money on him; therefore, thievery could not have been the motivation. He was a prominent and erudite person, respected both in the Jewish community in Damascus and Rome. The eyes and the mouth of the deceased were wide open, disfigured by the expression of horrible suffering. As no bodily injury or signs of physical harm were found, it was assumed that he died of heart-related causes. However, the doctors who examined the body were puzzled because his skin resembled that of the victims of drowning. In Damascus, with a soil that was mostly hard and firm, this failed to earn a reasonable explanation. The body of Don Mantino was given to the Jewish community for the burial, and the whole incident was soon forgotten.

It was in the year 5309, the tenth of Av, when the body of Don Mantino was buried in Damascus. Rabbi Joseph Taitazak had officiated at the funeral. The famed Gaon of Rome was taken down by angels in Syria. The night after the funeral, Rabbi Taitazak read the letter from Reb Yosimon of Prague one more time. Then, he burnt it and broke the fast of the ninth of Av that he always kept for two days. His heart rejoiced, and he had the quiet and restful sleep that night.

Jacob Mantino was the nemesis of Shlomo Molcho. The man plotted tirelessly, publicly and with less tact than would be expected from a prominent person and a member of the Jewish faith. It is not clear why and how he got to hate Rabbi Molcho, spy on him and finally turn the crown against the young Rabbi. The drive behind destructive emotions was not known, but was evidenced by the pieces of correspondence and those who witnessed the episodes of open hostility. It was cruel and unforgivable that he brought Shlomo Molcho into the hands of the Inquisition. Rav Yosimon followed young Rabbi on his adventures in Italy and was aware of the adversity but could not protect him. His grave was already commissioned by Jacob Mantino. The audience at the court confirmed what he expected. King's judgement was stern and finite. Charles V was challenged. Zealous souls are often blinded by the passion. The fire may illuminate the heart with the glory of heaven, yet it is dangerous to show the flame to the undeserving. If we do not flaunt our accomplishments in front of others, envy will not cause hate and anger to flare up. Humility is the invisibility cloak that protects from dangers. Molcho failed to use it. He could not subdue his passionate soul. He could not hide it from the evil eyes.

He lived and preached in times of little certainty and safety. Life resembled swimming through murky waters. One could be swallowed by dangerous whirlpools at any moment. Jews and ordinary gentile folk were at the mercy of their masters, who had little compassion but did not lack power over the lives of their subjects. Matters tried by the Inquisition were sometimes brought up for different reasons and blamed on the person out of pure hate or envy. Brevity and verbosity were not the best qualities for a Jew conversing with the Pope or a King. Shlomo Molcho employed all these qualities to his demise. Rav Yosimon tried to reason with Don Mantino, but his pleas were met with cold indifference. As the man of science and wealth, Mantino was completely uninterested in matters of mysticism and spiritual quests. He considered himself lucky to be out of Spain and in close relationship with Vatican. Pope Clement cherished understanding and respect for the Jewish faith. Then Shlomo Molcho appeared. A dangerous dreamer who could compromise volatile alliance between the church and Jewish community. He came when they found the respite from sword, fire, and murderous crowds of Spanish soldiers and peasants.

Summoning of the angels reminded Jacob Mantino of the concessions he had to accept to survive. He remembered those he left for the safety of Rome. The return of the second-generation marranos, stories of his fiery faith, circumcision, mysticism, brought back memories of auto d'feu, despair, and losses too great to bear.

The episode with David Reubeni was even more difficult to understand. Why did he chase and follow that Arab and impostor around? What kind of alliance was he trying to establish? Both Jews and Christians were blind to the pleas of Reubeni who lobbied for the impossible cause: an army against Ottoman Turks. Jews of Spain and Portugal in exile were tired and disillusioned.

Shlomo Molcho was a handsome man, too. Beauty is not a sin but can cause many. The wise know physical attraction can be more a cause for concern than joy. It inspires dangerous passions and often arouses and summons those we do not want nearby. At a critical moment, Shlomo Molcho failed to inspire compassion in those he approached with pleas for help. Unfortunately, he attracted the attention of those who could cause nothing but destruction.

Vittoria Colonna met Rabbi Molcho at the reception given by Pope Clement VII in his palace in Rome. She was a widow. She was religious. As a poet, and a muse to the greatest minds of the epoch, she was praised for her beauty, talent, and virtue. Vittoria was born into the family of aristocrats. She married a nobleman who spent most of his life in military campaigns; she found the consolation for the lonely days of her marriage and widowhood in writing poetry and praying on the isle of Ischia. The Pope and her brother wanted her to marry again. Her piety took a different path. The longing of the soul was for the higher realms. As the desire to surrender to the celestial powers grew stronger, her body weakened and faded.

Imagine the circumstances in the life of a young widow whose husband did not share her taste for elevated causes. He dies as an army commander accomplished and praised by the King whom he faithfully served for years. He leaves no children behind; the best time of his life he spent with his mistress. Still, despite being aware of the weaknesses of the deceased husband, a virtuous wife continues to compose sonnets, mourning and praising him in death. She is young, beautiful, wealthy, and powerful. People who shape the destiny of the entire nation listen and respect her opinion. Yet, she prays for the favour of Heaven. Her only passion is love for God.

The sole purpose of the existence of the soul is to praise its Creator. The soul is the spark sent to the body for a lifetime; it is the divine spark filled with longing for the heavenly realms. The lifetime lasts but a moment, and the soul rejoices in returning to purity; it dwells in the heavenly courts once again. The elevated souls are sent to those who learn and live by the laws known even before they are born. Vittoria Colonna recognized this soul while listening to the fiery words of the enlightened speaker. She perceived its depth and power. She failed to understand the message it carried.

There are secrets not admitted even to one's heart. Whether because of the inability to comprehend one's purpose or limitations of the intellect, some secrets remain locked deep in the mind's eye. It is a blessing given to a few—to see the purpose of the toils of the moment or the toils of the entire life before our last breath expires. Most often, the prayers we direct to our Creator are the cries of the soul we do not understand. The path leading to redemption is paved with loss, pain, and self-deception. The pain and desolation neither help nor speed up the journey each of us is supposed to take in our lifetime. What is the role of the prayers? They may conjure what we prayed for but cannot accept upon ourselves. Beware what you pray for.

Those who dwell in the celestial firmaments, strictly ordered by ranks and tasks, listen to our heartfelt prayers but have no grasp of the earthly boundaries. Those heavenly powers listened to Vittoria Colonna's prayers and glanced in her direction. They saw a young woman of childbearing age praising love, loyalty, and the Creator; touched by sincerity, they brought her near the kindred soul. The one who was full of love, light, and praise for the Creator: Shlomo Molcho. The marchioness was asking for the gift of being closer to God - the angels brought her close to Solomon Molcho, the Jew. Well, the angels understand only Hebrew of all languages; their names are in Hebrew, and they respond to them when summoned. Spiritual entities do not act in compliance with the laws of human societies. They just execute decisions of the higher powers. Words Shlomo spoke planted the seed that grew into a mighty tree. Those words also lit the fire on his gallows sometime later.

She was listening. She swallowed his shadow and locked the memory of his voice in her ear. Then she took the memory of his words, his face, smile and secretly worshipped it before sleep. The poetry could not console her, and prayers did not offer peace any longer. Thoughts of the brief meeting were the only consolation; the need to see him again filled her nights with dreams of hope; mornings brought despair of hopeless reality. She could not understand the overwhelming emotion; she could not explain the magnitude of the storm that left her desolate. Until that evening, Rosh Chodesh Elul, the life of Vittoria Colonna, resembled a beautiful painting hanging in a perfect balance of joy and sorrow. Despite the loss and suffering, she lived it well.

She lived her life well until Molcho walked into it. Vittoria heard him talk about the creation concepts in the poetry of The Bahir. Before this event, he had the reputation of a sorcerer; the speech on the Bahir upgraded it to a conspirator. His friendship with David Reubeni aroused suspicion and contempt. This should not have mattered to those present. However, everything mattered when it became clear what the message Molcho delivered in the palace of the Pope.

Vittoria Colonna and Shlomo Molcho shared a nightmare after their paths crossed. Her perception of reality was corrupted by arrogance; his intentions were mistaken for promises; hope was spoiled with lust; sobriety was replaced by vengeance. Reconciliation was no longer possible. Mercy gave a way to the stern judgement. The poet misunderstood hints sent by heaven. A brief meeting was supposed to inspire compassion. Instead, it aroused powers of destruction.

No matter how educated the gentiles were, one never knew when they would turn against the Jewish community, their observances, and learnings. There was not a single person of faith left untouched by Rabbi Molcho's sermon at the opening of the month of Elul. But the world often turns words spoken out of pure heart into a curse, not a blessing. One more time, sweet words of wisdom were used for grave accusations against the speaker. Maybe his intentions were not so pure after all, they speculated. He may have intended to deliver the message of peace and forgiveness. Alas, the message was taken for an insult. He spoke about the truth embedded in the easy-to-understand content of the scriptures. Within comparison of the two texts, he pointed at the errors in translation.

People seldom admit to the failure of the entire system of beliefs. If the system is a foundation for the institutions of power, the criticism will be rejected, censored, and destroyed at once. Those who dare challenging the established order are punished and perished.

Vittoria Colonna got entangled in the cobweb of questions without answers. The words of Solomon Molcho, convoluted, yet discernible, spoke of Christian observance and piety as poorly disguised, diluted, and ill-translated observance of the Jewish faith. Most of the learning of the Christians resulted from a lack of insight into deeper layers of the Hebrew text. Human beings have a dread of the unknown and resist stepping into unchartered territory. Little knowledge can fill us with hate for everyone and everything that could disturb

41

our delicate balance built on the comfort of the familiar circumstances. Vittoria Colonna tried to fight off the feeling of failure as a person of faith. She thought the goal could be accomplished if the Rabbi admitted he was at fault when he delivered the discourse on Christianity and Judaism. She sent the invitation asking him to visit her two weeks after the meeting in Pope's residence. The outcome of their conversation failed her expectations. She ended up shaken by his presence one more time and did not have any peace after he left. He was not trying to prove anything. Instead, while looking at her with the intensity that made her blush, he spoke further about ideas discussed in the Bahir. Rabbi outlined his view of the world and people of faith with carefully selected words. He said with determination:

'There are no people of faith except Jewish nation. Unification with the sefirot (emanations of God's presence) is not possible for gentiles. Marchioness's soul is placed in this world of darkness with a special purpose. Your passion is the evidence that though we have been scattered across the lands and seas for the longest time, we belong to the same seed. Once, we had been the same and one, filled with divine inspiration, protected by divine presence, standing close to the truth. Returning to that exact point in creation is the goal of all our striving. It will be achieved. The fulfilment of the prophecy may be full of perils but will be successful. It is unknown how many more will die for the cause. Yet, it is a cause worth dying for. Jewish people are placed in the world with one purpose: to lead humanity on the journey to the original creation corrupted by wrong choices. We prevented the light to prevail throughout. We were in a different place, named The Garden of Eden. Paradise. The place itself was neither a garden nor a paradise; it was the embodiment of

GODMIND that allowed its creation to mimic freedom of choice. In the aftermath, we were thrown away from the source of light and into the darkness of existence within the realms of the physical world.'

PART TWO

The Righteous Who Have Evil

Deep within, the stirred soul of Vittoria Colonna could not grasp the meaning of longing that got hold of her. Once left without the response, lust turned into vengeance. The lust for revenge is the mother of misery. We are engaged in a battle that would end in ultimate defeat. Trying to correct the mistakes while making all new ones.

If we keep trying hard to be heard, we may not hear what others are saying. Shlomo Molcho did everything to inspire. He wanted to make people think about the ideas that changed his life. He did not listen to the barking of enemies behind his back. He was looking for those who would help him fulfil his purpose. At first this was not clear. He saw the snarling face of a beast. The road ahead was tied into a knot. It was too late. He ran out of time before the completion of his quest. Vittoria Colonna, one of the most respected women of her epoch, the muse of the artists and the poet with connections among Vatican clergy, sided with the wolves.

'This I received from the tradition. When Moses wanted to know about the glorious fearsome Name, he said: Show me please Your glory (Exodus 33:18). He wanted to know why there are righteous who have good, righteous who have evil, wicked who have good, and the wicked who have evil. But they would not tell him... Why is there the righteous person who has good and another righteous person who has evil? This is because the second righteous person was wicked previously and is now being punished. I am not speaking of his present lifetime. I am speaking about what he has already been previously.' (Bahir, 195)

If the intentions are not recognised as hostile from the beginning, they are most likely introduced as genuine concern for the higher cause. Yet, they are evil. Our heroine embarked on a journey to the labyrinth of the Jewish community of Rome and those prominent members whose word echoed in both worlds: the ghetto and the influential catholic clerics. Approaching the right people who shared relevant information brought the Inquisition onto the stage. It was confirmed by the events that resulted in Molcho's incineration that it was always easier to find allies to destroy one's life than save it. Don Mantino was one of the community leaders during those times. He knew suffering, and those who suffered. He witnessed the disarray after the expulsion, life in fear, poverty, and despair. There had been so much cruelty caused by the gentiles; who believed more could be caused by a fellow Jew?

Gabriel Marcus spent the evening going through the drawings that Prof. Vasiliadis gave him. One drawing was laminated and attached to many pages of notes. They explained the inscriptions of the Cabalistic square, made by Molcho or his teacher, Rabbi Taitazak. The drawing was in the suitcase with papers, photographs, and other notes. It was a plan of the sanctuary of the Temple. The notes were dealing with the incense service; thoughts, facts, work of the day when it was recorded. One paragraph was a commentary on the order of the service; this was followed by the list of the ingredients used to compound the formula. The long list of ingredients was attached. Other notes recorded the discussion on the timeline of the events to usher the messianic era. Professor pointed at some names that stated that could have been the reason Shlomo Molcho fell out of grace in the Jewish community and was labelled a self-proclaimed messianic candidate. Jacob Mantino considered him dangerous because he shared his ideas and what he learned. Thus, even though Shlomo Molcho never claimed to be the anointed one, he shared knowledge that was secret and forbidden. Many scholars of Jewish mysticism think this explained his early, tragic end. The events leading to the arrest by the Inquisition were the result, not the cause of his demise.

The Birth

In the year 5293, Rosh Chodesh Kislev, Vered Zemora arrived in Damascus to stay in the home of the relatives of Rabbi Joseph Taitazak. She had no family to go to. It was the most welcoming place in the world to her. Vered Zemora was at the last stage of pregnancy when she arrived in Damascus. She was glad to leave Tsfat behind. Tsfat was the place of solitude and desperation. For many weeks she had been waiting for her husband's return from Rome. She was watching the hazy horizons with a line between eyebrows that made her face look older; worry made her retreat deeper into silence. She knew he would never come back. The last memory she cherished was the cheerful conversation they shared at the dawn of his departure. They were standing at the door, and his travelling companions were already waiting. He kissed and held her for a long time, tried to disperse sadness. He would be back in four months. Then he quietly stared into her eyes. No words were exchanged, and none were needed. She understood well what he would say. He was already saying it in silence. He was thrilled with the news about the baby. They spent more time together in the first weeks of pregnancy. Shlomo was always by her side and helped with all kinds of chores and errands.

During the short time they spent together until he embarked on that last journey, she got to love him dearly. She was never so happy. The pregnancy and the child growing inside made her feel complete and strong. Somehow, she knew this would not last. Every day was perfect. Every hour was bright and pure as cast in silver. Shlomo was a gentle and kind soul, deeply devoted and honest. She felt blessed just for being in his presence. The bad news, however, did not arrive unexpectedly. Nobody hoped anything good would come out of his adventure in Italy. His future was decided the moment he returned to the faith of his ancestors, was sealed when he advocated for the war with Turks; Many could attest to the accusation of summoning angels by pronouncing their names. The names that must not be uttered. He stood alone and spoke, but people could neither hear nor understand what he said. His entire life resembled walking through the crowds yet standing alone. The crown of martyrdom was the foreseeable ending to it all. What a horrible way to die! Yet, Vered Zemora did not feel he died. His presence, warmth, and kindness filled the room as if he never left. Weeks after death, she would think about his return home and had to remind herself he would not. The news of the execution reached her in Damascus. She had not any strength left for despair. Vered gave birth to a beautiful baby girl. The child had sapphire blue eyes and a glow of peace on the face.

Gabriel Marcus was packing his suitcase again. He included all precious items for his trip to Israel. He planned and booked the lodging in Tel- Aviv and Jerusalem. He finally scheduled the meetings and tours. Many were cancelled ahead of his arrival. Upon the cancellations, he was filled with the joy as a student whose test was suddenly postponed. He could go play games in the schoolyard. Gabriel learned to relax and enjoy the trip as an adventure. Having spent months working on a research project and attempts to get in touch with several people, this was a much-needed change, and he enjoyed it with a full heart. Very few scholars were familiar with his family heirloom. The research involving cabbalistic texts was usually of no interest to historians. Curiosity invested in the family's past took a different direction altogether and outgrew his ability to achieve progress alone.

The attempts to contact Torah scholars immersed in studies of Kabbala were equally frustrating and made him realise he had no choice but to pack and head to Israel. People he needed to talk to did not communicate by emails. It was impossible to get in touch by phone, either. For the sake of his project, he had to continue the quest in Israel. He dedicated some time to work with Aviva Baumstein, a historian from the Museum of Diaspora. She specialised in communities coming from Portugal and Spain. A brief visit to Tsfat was just for sentimental reasons and a visit to the cemetery. He hoped to stay the longest in Jerusalem, at the yeshiva of Beth-El. The leader of that community was a Torah scholar, a cabbalist, acclaimed expert, well versed in the content of his suitcase; the excitement that followed this decision was enormous. After all, he returned to the place where the initial events in the life of his ancestors unfolded. Thoughts of the journey to Tsfat filled him with childish curiosity.

He could hardly wait to visit the cemetery, synagogues, the art colony that turned the labyrinth of narrow streets and steps into a vibrant community of artists and chassids. Complete tranquillity took over his whole being. Past, present, and future were the part of a continuous flow emanating from here and now. He could feel himself in the present moment and understand its weight and value.

As he was closing the suitcase, the laminated parchment slid out of the pile and his eyes locked on the inscriptions in Hebrew that filled the page. The letters flashed with black flame before him. They lifted and circled in the uninterrupted line just as they were inked onto the parchment. They danced in front of him as living beings. The words from the book of Numbers 10: 35,36 were inscribed on it: When the Ark went forth, Moses said: Arise, G-d and scatter your enemies. Let your foes flee before you. When it came to rest, he said: return, G-d, the myriads of Israel's thousands.

This too filled him with tremendous joy and zeal to continue his quest.

Sambuca Latte

He landed in Tel Aviv, the city with beautiful and loud people filling the streets and strolling along the boardwalk. The first two days of the visit were dedicated to the archives of the Diaspora Museum. He embarked on a search for the migration records with passion. The data on the exodus from Spain and Portugal were nothing he had not known. He accomplished little and was about to resign his quest and head to Jerusalem when Aviva finally agreed to their meeting. She had cancelled their rendezvous twice before because of some urgent family matters. Instead of greeting him at the airport, as scheduled, a man holding the sign with his name silently took his luggage into the car and drove him to the hotel. There were two more apologies over two days for events planned after his arrival. She promised to make herself available when she returns to the city. His first days in the Land were not going as expected. Then, Aviva phoned and asked how long it may take him to include her in his schedule for the rest of the day. They met at the boardwalk café on a sticky summer evening.

Aviva was a woman that people would remember not for the beauty of her facial features, but a strong and confident demeanour and pleasant attitude when she conversed. She has been with the archives of the Museum for a few years and completed extensive research on the Sephardi population and their communities. Her job was to manage the file that contained all documents the Israeli government got and stored. It was the largest resource of information on migrations of the population after expulsions from Spain and Portugal. Being the best person to consult on tracing the ancestry links to the shattered and scattered lot of Spanish Jewry, she was much sought after and had little time to spend at semi-private meetings with people who had requests for help with filling the gaps in their family histories. Gabriel Marcus deserved special attention. It was not only because he was the descendant of a famous progenitor, the one considered a martyr for the faith, but because of dedication, and the intensity of emotions vested into his project.

Based on legends and a couple of receipts issued in the name of his famous ancestor for the goods purchased in Tsfat, there was nothing that would connect him to the land. Not a single document was found to evidence the birth of Rabbi Molcho's child or the proof that his wife ever existed. The baby was born in Damascus and Vered Zemora lived in Tsfat for only a year before she met and got wedded to the Rabbi. Aviva gathered everything that could be used in closing the gap between Damascus and Auschwitz. She spent days going through the records before she met Gabriel and was ready to unfold the meagre fruit of her work. Most of it was echoing the story forwarded by Prof. Vasiliadis. Yet, everything was compiled, organized, and labelled in a way to be used in any future endeavour. The latest results of the research were as two notes and receipts -the only proof of Shlomo Molcho's brief existence in Israel.

They were sitting in the cafe near the beach over empty cups of espresso and pastries that had to be guarded against the persistent attacks of the angry bees. As the metallic blue of the sky was turning into blazing colours of the sunset, the air felt like a hot, damp blanket pressed against the skin. Gabriel had difficulty breathing in humidity and dust from traffic. He tried to relax and not think about the heat. Aviva was calm and stared into the fireworks of colours and shades on the western horizon. After an hour spent in a conversation with Gabriel, she was looking for an excuse to leave. She lacked the strength to get up and wiggle her way out of the crowded boardwalk. The man sitting opposite her at the table seemed lost in his thoughts. Gabriel was gazing at the sunset and made no comments about her notes or any work she had done so far. They were sliding silently into the night.

'I know a place that is less crowded than the beach. It is cool and serves decent Sambuca latte. Or we can just call it a night and meet again to continue our discussion,'- suggested Aviva.

Aviva thought it was not much of a discussion and wondered if their future meeting would take them further into the investigation of the whereabouts of Shlomo Molcho's decedents. There was something about Gabriel's forlorn gaze that swayed in the back of her mind and made her stay. She felt that he desperately needed help. At that moment, Aviva B. was compelled to respond to this muted cry for help. She sensed he did not need her for the research in the archives while pondering over the ancestry connections. He was completely and utterly alone and lonely. She could perceive the abyss that no one surmounted before. He did not relate to anyone in this vast world and was isolated and walled off from the people by the uniqueness of his existence. The past. The present. The future.

Are we not all? Unique? Lonely in our intricate designs with so many tiny facets reflecting the light from within? Is she not built the same way, with the same flaws and thorns pointed at the world? Aviva Baumstein had dark shadows filling her soul, too. In the years of her adolescence, she seldom broke the silence to express her opinions, feelings, wishes. She was leery of the strangers and seldom acknowledged the existence of those who shared 'here' and 'now' with her, anywhere. It took a long time to earn her trust, even longer to bring a smile to her face. This typical humid Tel-Aviv evening made her irritable. However, she made an exception and stayed. The sky at the west had turned the display of dramatic colours into dark velvet above the still water. They were sitting in the cafe off Ben Yehuda Street, in the room that was cool and dark enough, so they could keep to their thoughts while sipping on Sambuca with three coffee beans floating in the glass for health, happiness, and prosperity.

Aviva Baumstein was the grandchild of the Zionists who built this city—people overflowing with enthusiasm for erecting the steel and glass towers out of the marshes previously home to mosquitos, reeds, and cattails. Nothing but complete devotion and pure faith in cause could have inspired the miraculous advancement of the country that raised like a phoenix from the sand. Aviva would love to share in the energy of Ben Gurion's generation but was born many years later and have seen the trajectory of the shooting star getting lost in the darkness.

She could not find her niche in this city, neither felt more at home elsewhere. Aviva was not alone, but wherever she went, her loneliness followed, the burden always on her shoulders; a songbird silenced by cruel captivity. Being a loner, she related and crossed the path with those that were in her likeness, locked within their minds, unable to communicate messages of sorrow, pain, or joy to the world or themselves. Unlike many of her peers, she was uncertain about her purpose in this world and understood little about herself and others.

Gabriel Marcus did not surprise her with his equally silent mind, perplexed manner of going about his affairs and inability to state the goal of his decisions. He travelled from afar to the land; By the measure of his accomplishments, the journey reached beyond his willpower and physical strength and resembled a built-in imperative of the flocks that migrate south every winter. The instinct, not reason or emotion, ran him about in the attempt to cross the oceans of time to an unknown destination. She could not but show admiration for his courage in pursuing the query, for reliving the memory long forgotten and left behind with nothing more than moonlight above the desolate landscape of his travels.

That night, two lonely ships were gleaming in the moonlight's silver. Aviva and Gabriel did not have to speak to each other. Their silence was conversing in the languages of the souls that lived in the land since the beginning of time.

Interruption

He could not understand the interruption in the ritual's order that took place every day of the year. The steps were set, and every little detail counted, but the meaning of the break in the flow of the 'work' puzzled him. He pondered over the scriptures for many hours, trying to understand the logic of the interruption, but was not progressing in the right direction.

The cleaning of the five lamps precedes the dashing of the blood of the continual offering; the blood of the continual offering precedes the cleaning of the other two lamps; the cleaning of the lamps precedes the burning of the incense.

There were seven lamps altogether, and they were cleaned in the order of five plus two. Cleaning was preceded by the removal of the ashes from the altar and followed by the burning of the incense. All steps have the logical flow in the schedule of the offerings throughout the day. This order is adopted from the writings of Rabbi Shaul and canonized as part of the morning prayers. It all makes perfect sense except for the interruption in the cleaning of the lamps to dash off the blood of the sacrifice. Why? He was thinking about the wicks placed in the pure olive oil used for the menorah; the branches made of gold and the care for the lights that was the daily duty of the High Priest and no other. Every single step had to be performed with unwavering accuracy. The service was even more stringent and elaborate on Yom Kippur. On that day, the High Priest would complete every step not only as part of the Temple service but add the one acting on behalf of the entire nation. He was the nation of Israel, standing in repentance for committed transgressions. It is the day when all actions, words, and intentions of the year in passing were scrutinised with judgement exacted over a hairbreadth. Some High Priests did not live up to expectations of the day. They died and had to be dragged from the chamber with the rope tied around their waist. The rope was employed because no one else was supposed to step into the Holy of Holies. On the last morning of his life, Shlomo Molcho was thinking about the interruption of the five plus two. Blood of the sacrifice dashed after cleaning five lamps, cleaning the remaining two lamps, then burning the incense on the altar.

Eleven different spices were mixed to make the unique formula of the incense: stacte, onycha, galbanum, frankincense, myrrh, cassia, spikenard, saffron, costus, aromatic bark, cinnamon. Yet the compounding process included more: Carshina lye, Cyprus wine, Sodom salt and Maaleh Ashan, a smoke raising herb. Adding or replacing any ingredient would invalidate the formula. No ingredient could have been left out. The one who would violate the process by changing anything in the mixture or the quantities was liable to death penalty. The ingredients in exact amount and proportions, as well as the compounding process, were known only to the priestly family serving the Temple. It remains a secret to the present day. Over centuries that followed the destruction of the second Temple, no one could agree on the names of the spices in the formula. They could not relate them to specific plants. No one knows where they were harvested, too.

Galbanum

Gabriel and Aviva were reclining in the bar in the late hours of the night. The glasses with blue-coloured liquid were on the table in front of them. The room was illuminated by dimmed light thrown sparingly by the wall scones. Gabriel was staring at his glass with sambuca fascinated by its hue. Anise that oozed with a sweet fragrance belonged to the same Umbellifers family as galbanum. Was anise one ingredient in the formula used for the Temple service? He reached out and grasped Aviva's hand, who in return looked at him with the expression of mixed surprise and fear. Yet, she did not withdraw her hand.

'Anise is galbanum, he repeated his thoughts aloud and looked at Aviva.'

She could not understand what he was talking about and raised her eyebrows in surprise. A few moments passed in expectation of a response. Gabriel was searching for words, but all good ones escaped him. Finally, he said something about the ingredients of the cocktail and complimented the taste of anise one more time. Then, in a hardly audible whisper and while staring at the floor, he mentioned that his mother knew a lot about the healing properties of the plants.

'It was more than an interest or a hobby. I was an asthmatic as a child, and treatments known to the conventional medicine were of little help. My mother spent many hours learning about the herbs and trying to find the right formula that could ease the condition that kept her awake at my bedside throughout many nights for the first ten years of my life. She mentioned anise as one herb that could ease breathing. I did not know it could be used as a food colour.'

'You had asthma, too?'- she asked, not being able to hide astonishment.

Aviva's look changed from surprise to curiosity and completely shifted her interest in the stranger that she found dull only an hour ago. She was sipping on tea made from anise and other herbs all her childhood and tried to recall other herbs that were included in the liquorice tasting liquid that she had to stomach a few times a day whenever she had the onset of wheezing and cough. Her asthma was getting worse, and the family had to move from Tel-Aviv to Tsfat. She spent five years of her childhood there, which resulted in the family break-up and domino effect of calamities around those dear to her heart.

She remembered the town in the Galilee for green hills and long walks. She used to take strolls through the shopping district and the cemetery. Tsfat was away from the main lifeline that connected Jerusalem, Tel-Aviv, and to a lesser extent, Tiberias. It was the home to a few religious families of Jews and a mostly dwindling Arab population. Nowadays, it has grown into an art colony, a trendy spot for any artisan inspired by Jewish mysticism. It became an important centre of Hasidism. Whether for the proximity of Meron with the tomb of Rabbi Shimon Ben Yochai, or the memories of the brief sojourn of Rabbi Luria and his disciples in the city, Tsfat has become a busy, crowded, and desired destination for many Jewish pilgrims and other adventurers on their travels through the Land.

Aviva has had her favourite tree near her old Tsfat home. She lived on Ha Nasi Street and enjoyed spacious yard that was in stark contrast to the alleyways, tunnels, and other labyrinth-like quarters of the old town. From her home, she often strolled to the tomb of Nachum Ish

Gamzu, even though she knew nothing about him. The grounds around the grave were grassy, shaded, and quiet, and she felt safe there. In those days, all she wanted was to be invisible; tuft of grass by the path, a whiff of cool air at the entrance of the tomb of Rabbi Gamzu. She could enjoy quiet solitude in this place on most days.

Aviva was the only child born late to her parents. She was the grandchild of the Holocaust survivors on her father's side. He told her the stories of five war years that robbed her bubby and zeidy of dreams and hopes. Five years they spent in daily struggles for survival that hinged on their ability to be invisible. They had to stay at a safe distance from murderers. Those were five years of living in squalor, hunger, fear, cold. They believed in the miracle of this country that rose over and over from the ashes of destruction. Aviva's father was the only child to those who anchored the ship in the early years of the state of Israel. He married her mother, the only child of the Moroccan Jews who were thrown out of their home when the state of Israel was announced. Aviva's mother was a gentle, yet physically robust woman. She had dark eyes, long hair that waived down the shoulders in black slopes, highlighting the pale complexion of the face. She was not beautiful, yet people would not forget the deep gaze of her eyes and her soft voice. Aviva could not imagine a person gentler and more understanding than her mother. Whenever she conjures the memories of her, she feels illuminated by her smile, loving eyes and beautiful voice singing: Durme, Durme, the old lullaby in Ladino going like this:

> 'Sleep, sleep; mother's little girl
> Free from worry and pain,
> Free from worry and pain.

On nights when Aviva did not feel well and could not fall asleep, she would sit next to her and repeat the above lyrics over and over until she had to whisper from exhaustion. It worked like magic. The singing would stop the spasmodic breathing and wheezing, and Aviva would get a much-needed rest. Her father was not around during the Tsfat years. He had to stay in Tel-Aviv and take care of his career and support the family. She saw him once a month, on weekends, and on some holidays. Therefore, the most memorable moments of her childhood were filled with her mother's presence and long walks around the neighbourhood. In time, she got better, and asthma attacks receded until they stopped altogether when she was ten.

'I was ten when my asthma subsided, too. I got my life back. I could do sports, travel, and visit my friends. Beforehand, everything was a peril. Every step I made, any vacation we planned. We could travel nowhere, as I got sick often. The attacks were violent. It was hard on my parents, too.'

Aviva continued to tell him about her family, her childhood, with the gush of words that came after the quiet start of their rendezvous. She did not feel awkward and distant anymore, and what she brought up during this conversation did not make her cringe when she reflected upon the events of the evening. The words came naturally and were received with perfect empathy and respect. The gentle kiss from this stranger also was not out of place when he saw her off to her car and wished her pleasant dreams. He did not ask for anything else and never interrupted her with words during the long discourse over the glasses of sambuca. It was only in the eyes; his eyes lit up with endless warmth and compassion, as if they were watching over her during all the years brought back in scattered memories. They re-lived their childhood pains in one hazy summer night.

Aviva wrote to Gabriel later, reminiscing on their first meeting:

'Plants may render more than we would deliberately disclose. They can reveal our inclinations, fears, and life purpose. They are all but innocent bystanders in decoding the secrets of the soul. Anything sophisticated seldom withstands the challenges of time. We will either grow and change or disappear with the disruption of our environment. You and I are children that grew like gentle, trembling threads of grass. We were tended by subtle forces of love and care of our mothers and treated by the healing juices of the plants. We reached adulthood but still tremble while standing alone in crowds of people and firm in belief that intellect and refined thinking make us stand out as human beings. I have often realised that subtlety and refinement lack in vitality and smell of death.'

Katarina Glozic

Pancratium Maritimum

Ischia is an island in the Gulf of Naples with the history dating from Roman times. Nowadays, it is famous for the Aragonese Castle built by the Marquis of Pescara in the fifteenth century. The landscape of the island is dominated by Mount Epomeo. For many seasons, this was home to Vittoria Colonna. The enchanting beauty of nature, mild weather, and warm soil harbouring rare and fragrant plants could do nothing but inspire the verses written to celebrate love, faith, and the family of the poetess.

> *'O when the tender breeze and my sweet light*
> *Made beautiful during the day, and pure and clear.*
> *The air, by paths, secure in daring flight.*
> *I sought to raise myself on wings from here.'*

She used to spend days walking the steep path to the ruins on the top of the Mount Epomeo. The hilly landscape of the island, with unique and luscious herbs, made Ischia into the enchanted garden and a shelter from the temptations of life in Rome. Poetess felt at home here, heart filled with peace, face touched by the warm sea breeze. The ever-green slopes of Epomeo with the ruins of the temple dedicated to Neptune were the perfect surrounding for healing the soul deeply immersed in sadness. She was living alone, far from her husband, even before he died. Eventually, she was widowed. In those times the society was entangled in warmongering, unrest, and discords.

> *'Helpless, in vain, in vain doth lift its gaze.*
> *I tarry here below for mortal pain.*
> *Defeating, I still live but loveless, alone,*
> *The while thought soared where my Sun doth reign.'*

Vittoria could have married again and was much sought after by those who reigned and changed the course of history. She declined all offers. Not for the sake of the memory of her dead husband; they were more apart than any good marriage would take. He neglected her. Nothing she did would make him love her. For the duration of their union, she was on Ischia while he was away at war or captivity. There was neither kindness nor gratitude for what she encountered to have him ransomed and help him become the army commander trusted by the Charles V. It was her family that paid the hefty ransom demanded by the French; it was she who tended to his wounds, if they had to be healed. Yet he never loved her.

Paths on Epomeo were more suitable for the goats than human feet. Light and exuberant, Vittoria skipped from one rock to another as if they were a stairway. The destination of advancing up the narrow path was the plateau where the ancient ruins once stood. The temple dedicated to the god of the seas was eventually turned into the church dedicated to the saint protector of the D'Avalos family; the edifice was molded into the volcanic rock, built with green tuff the island is famous for among the craft workers and masons.

Vittoria would ascend here to lodge her prayers daily. The sanctuary was the closest place to the skies above Ischia. Yet the skies were closed to her prayers. This is something that she will understand much later, after the carefree days of the first year of her marriage were over.

In those days of their unity, life seemed bright and promising. Fernando made sure she woke up with the bouquet of sand lilies in her room. Sometimes he would pick the flowers and bring them himself. They were blooming in the sandy areas of the island and filled the air with delicate scent. Sand lily is a plant native to the

Mediterranean beaches and coastal dunes. It got the name because most of its leaves grow under the sand. Nowadays, it is on the verge of extinction across the region; the sand lily, or sand daffodil or Pancratium Maritimum is pollinated by a hawk moth. This quiet plant philander can fly only at the speed of wind under two meters per second. Sand lily is not receptive to its own pollen and must be cross-pollinated. The hawk moth, gentle as the breeze that carries it to the flowers, is sensitive to pollution, change in temperature and not likely to survive harsh weather. Neither the flower nor the moth could adapt to the changes in the environment.

The memories of people, their joys, and pains fade. Memories of Vittoria Colonna, the Marchioness of Pescara, and her shadow on the shores of Ischia faded. They are vivid in the sonnets of the gifted young woman imbued with passion. They are crowned by her piety and love for art. Long ago her name was mentioned with awe. She was a muse of the eminent artists, a wife to the army commander, and a role model in her generation. The memories are like leaves and flowers pressed into herbarium. They are preserved in hope to surmount the challenges of transiency. The memories of a dead dreamer that reverberate with failed expectations. They fade. Hawk moth dreaming of dead sand lilies.

Fernando D'Avalos consumed women like wine. He thought of women and wine with the same spark in the eye, same thirst on his palate. Like Lambrusco, refreshing and tasting of berries, some women are light and agreeable and can be enjoyed at any hour and on any day. Others should be consumed only on certain occasions. They unravel slowly but are admired for the fullness of their soul, as well as the taste of their lips. Those that should be taken seriously are usually a fortunate mixture of unique qualities that complement the shortcomings of their mates in the most flattering way: satisfying the lasting desire, fulfilling the hidden hope, dispersing the shameful fears. They are the accomplices in the battles that are not recorded in any of the chronicles. They are what men identify as soulmates and women as the crafty ones.

Vittoria was neither of the above. Fernando D'Avalos has not had the key that would unlock the heart of his wife and has not aspired to find one. His eyes were gazing into the horizon, trying to make out the colour of the moon when it lit up in the night sky and contemplated only what the next day would bring about; and most of his days were lived as a tribute to death. He did not need love in his life. Vittoria had not given him the heir and failed to conceive in all years of their marriage. She has not been of any use to him. Failing to produce the legitimate posterity, Marquis of Pescara has resumed what suited him best: warmongering. When he took a prominent role in the Italian wars, he seldom returned to visit his wife. Until the battle of Ravenna, he was praised for his strength and endurance. Then he was wounded and made captive. Had he been blessed with wisdom; he would have understood that some wounds never stop bleeding. They open many years even after we treat them. They have the power to call upon us all kinds of fresh injuries and scars. Nine years after the battle of Ravenna, Fernando D'Avalos was wounded again and never recovered. He died in Milan at the closing of the year 1525. Vittoria Colonna was not there to lay her hands on the eyes of her dying husband. The news of his last moments found her on the road to the place where he was recuperating from injuries and weakness.

'I was ordered to set on a journey to be at my husband's deathbed. We have not been in each other's company for two months short of a year. I cannot remember the colour of his eyes or the way he walks. Tragically, he is going to die young. Waging wars has been taxing on his strength, and it has been a while since he could mount a horse without an expression of pain on his face. That is how I remember him: leaving in full armour to fight in the battle of Pavia. I am summoned to the deathbed of a man that did not love me, was not faithful to me, gave me no children. Am I supposed to grieve? Is he going to ask me to don a monastic robe on myself after his death? I do not grieve for his life, nor his presence, for I had no pleasure to have him by my side for a long time. He never loved me. Am I supposed to grieve for someone who acknowledged my existence as the embodiment of duty he had to fulfil by becoming a husband? Why did he summon me to travel from Rome to Milan to spend a few hours on his deathbed? He knows I would not be mourning his death even if I had drowned myself in tears. The grief for what we desired but never had is more difficult to endure than cry over the lost possession of a physical body. We were not kindred souls, and I never found consolation for any of my sorrows while by his side. He never loved me.'

Vittoria Colonna never made it to deliver this farewell to her dying husband. He passed away before she reached Milan on December 3rd, 1525. However, rare souls with longing for heaven can grieve for what has never been. Vittoria Colonna will transform the bitterness of her early widowhood into sweet sonnets about love, loyalty, and beauty. She became the muse of the artists and the friend of the poets. They praised her for her piety, simplicity, and honesty. Then she met Shlomo Molcho. Her life changed, but she could not cry about it or compose verses to preserve the memory of those times. It was her dark secret, one to be ashamed of, never shared with a living soul. The most precious secret. One of those that are shared with heaven only by the way of thoughts and silent prayers; never whispered or written. This secret stirred the feelings that had awoken her whole being and made her question the roots of her existence. It brought illness upon her. Once the infirmity set, it never left her side but hovered above as a malevolent spirit till the end of her time. Vittoria saw the abyss filled with frightening whispers that forever poisoned the joy of life and snarled at her viciously from the mirror.

Tsfat

Aviva spent a day trying to make sense of the last night. She had to admit that it changed her secluded, mostly self-sufficient existence. She did not want to go back to her garden inside the tall walls. For years, she has been trying hard to build those walls, a fence without the gate, tested it for weaknesses, certain that nothing would breach it. Occasionally, there were people she met that would attempt to get inside but would give up and move on after a few unsuccessful trials. Gabriel Marcus just kissed her and wished her a peaceful night; she was excited as an innocent schoolgirl and went over that evening over and over in her thoughts. It was not the attraction that connected them; She did not find him attractive; Gabriel was clumsy and quiet, thoughtful, caring, a contraption of her desires, the reality that cannot be denied; someone that most people would call destiny.

Aviva did not believe in destiny, but she believed in her instincts, the call from the dark realm of the memories that were not only hers but echoed the existence of all souls that related to her through passages of time; the whispers that told her to listen and follow the map. That voice within told her she was about to take on a steep path. Gabriel would make her company.

Only when she closed the door behind her, Aviva realised she had not asked him anything in return for sharing her memories. She filled their evening by talking about her. She looked forward to their next meeting to take on the role of a listener.

Gabriel walked a little longer along the boardwalk; then headed to the hotel. He had to wake up early the next morning and will join the driver and enjoy the ride to Tsfat. He will spend a few days walking around the town and hills, reminiscing, enjoying the peace of the Galilee and try to re-live the memory of his famous ancestor's visit to the place many centuries ago. Yet he did not know where to start his journey, and the whole idea seemed more enticing while he was sitting with Aviva in the bar. He did not believe that providence would lead him on this adventure and sent the message as soon as he reached the hotel: 'Please meet me in Safed. A weekend together? I cannot imagine a better guide than you.'

There was no response to his message later, and in the morning. After they drove to Tsfat, he was taken by a quick and profound change in landscape and stopped thinking about last night or Aviva. As the road was heading to the hills, palms and reeds gave way to herbaceous shrub and pine trees. The air was fresh at the higher grounds and sunlight jumped off the limestones. The haze of humid Tel-Aviv disappeared, and the heat was easier to bear. He asked the driver to stop frequently to take pictures or simply enjoy part of the scenery that spread out on the sides of the road. As the winding route to Tsfat was about to end, Gabriel grew more excited and somewhat felt lighter. The sign informed them about the last turn towards the destination; he felt as if he was coming home. He wanted the visit to be an adventure and did not make any bookings. The phone calls did not precede his arrival, and no itineraries or tours were scheduled. No one was to expect his arrival on this day and hour. He wanted to explore and enjoy every moment of his stay, undisturbed by the ideas of other people. Gabriel wanted to go about town and think of the additional steps to take and unknown places to visit, as they attract his attention. However, at the end of the drive, all that he could think of was last night and Aviva. He checked his inbox again and again for her message.

There was a café that looked like a perfect place for the late breakfast, and he entered. While sipping on his coffee in the shade of the limestone walls, he could not shrug off persistent, curious stare of the only other guest at the table next to his. The man did not take the eyes off Gabriel all the time while he was eating. He walked in shortly after Gabriel arrived. The staring face-off was going on for ten or fifteen minutes until Gabriel reproached the curious pair of eyes locked on his coffee. He tried to sound composed and calm, but his stomach was tied into a knot and muscles trembled from tension:

'I am sorry... but could not help noticing interest invested in my food and everything I have been doing since you stepped into the room. Is there a reason for this? ', his tone was harsh and alarmed; after all, he was determined to get rid of this person before he ruined his day. The man was not disturbed by the question or the tone and eager to start the conversation himself. He said:

'I could help you find a place where the house was. It is no more. But I know the exact spot....'

'Excuse me?' Gabriel was shocked by the direction of the conversation more than anything he had experienced since the beginning of his journey. More than the chain of the events of last night and his arousing feelings for Aviva. For a few moments, he was reluctant to respond or even look at the stranger. 'If I continue on this path,' he thought, 'I will just go through the rabbit hole. I do not want to go that way.'

Have you ever been standing on both sides of the mirror? If you have, you are probably not counted among the living. This is exactly how Gabriel felt during the event that took place on that morning in Tsfat. He realised that no matter how unusual and unwanted the experience was, it could not have been undone; he could not pretend it did not happen. Ignoring the offer would have solved nothing. Therefore, he made the only likely choice and took a challenge from the conversation. He said in a shrill and trembling voice:

'Excuse me? Are you sure I am the right person to talk to about your offer, whatever that may be?'

'You came to find out more about Rabbi Molcho, his wife, his child, no?'

Few moments in Gabriel's life deserve to be remembered and preserved until the end of his time; this was one of them. He was reviewing any past connection to this man: pale face with the beard, white, plain cap, glasses on top of a finely shaped nose. He tried to recall any messages that he may have forgotten that resulted in this encounter. There were none. No rational explanation for the man with the white cap staring at him and offering help with his personal and unannounced quest in Tsfat. The stranger came out of thin air and seemed to have the ability to read his mind. Gabriel was gaping for a few moments and did not respond. He was searching for the right words and tried to conceal the shock that his face reflected. Maybe this took too long, maybe he looked too surprised by the offer and the man stood up, put a piece of paper on the table and left the restaurant. Gabriel looked at the note with the phone number and the name Yossi. No last name.

All he wanted at that moment was to forget about the encounter. He tried to banish any thoughts about the stranger he just met in the café on Ha Ari street. Gabriel did not want to read into the incident as a sign. His mother told him on an occasion:

'Gab, do not make signs for signs...' he did not understand if this was supposed to be taken as a piece of advice or the rebuke; here, it could be understood as a warning not to get derailed by occasional mysteries on his life journey. He could have found at least a dozen rational explanations for the appearance of a strange man in the café. He will rest and think about it later; Should he use the phone number shoved into his hand or consider? He could not decide at that moment.

The hotel located a few steps away seemed decent. He took a room there and stared at the walls with the shades closed and lights off for the rest of the afternoon. Gabriel must have fallen asleep; when he opened the window, the sun had already set. He experienced the sudden arrival of the night that differed from a hazy dusk of Tel-Aviv. Aviva messaged him. She would join him on Friday morning and spend Shabbat in Tsfat. His heart filled with warm, sweet peace. Happiness and anticipation of their reunion made him jump through the winding passages and alleyways of the old town the next morning. Anticipation of the meeting turned him into a mighty warrior. Conquering the steep stairways was the only goal of the day and he took upon it with renewed enthusiasm.

Onycha

On the second day in town, he turned on to the road encircling the cemetery and strolled down to the blue-painted tombstones of those that made this place stand out on the map. Gabriel spent some time looking at the inscriptions in Hebrew, navigated around many visitors who prayed, walked, or just quietly stood paying their respect. His attention passed from the people and tombs to the shrubbery that fired with his fuchsia-coloured flowers at the passers-by. Among the scarce greenery on the hillside, he recognised the rock rose as its rich, enticing fragrance tickled his nostrils even before he spotted the flowers. The flower would open and wave its petals for a single day and die the next. This would take place several times during the blooming season; the plant would continue to push out flowers throughout the summer. He stopped and inhaled the fragrance. When he returned to the same spot the next morning, the flowers were already gone. 'The plant could be onycha,' Gabriel whispered for himself, looking at the shrub that had shut its fragrant pink display and was sitting silently in its luscious greenery. Nothing of value for the bouquet. He grinned at the shrub and returned to the marketplace to purchase a bottle of wine for him and Aviva instead of flowers.

As he was buying the wine in a store tucked into the mosaic of windows and doors of the Art Colony, he spotted the man from the café again. He did not pay any attention to him and seemed engaged in his own business, but the possibility of a meeting alarmed Gabriel. He spun around and left the area. When Aviva phoned to announce she was close, he forgot about running into Yossi. Aviva was waiting in front of the hotel, smiling, radiant and beautiful. She reminded him of the flower in the wild rose shrubbery he admired the day before.

Aviva took him to another part of the commercial district, the place she frequently visited when in town, while he was telling her about the episode with the stranger. He skipped the latest event during his walk around the town. He was silent on the conflicting thoughts hunting him since the encounter in the cafe. Gabriel felt discouraged about retracing the steps of Shlomo Molcho in Tsfat. He was not sure what he was looking for anymore. How could he expect to find the footage of someone who lived in town for a short time a few hundred years ago? No one kept the records of marriages and births in the sixteenth century Tsfat. Many desperate souls reached the borders of the Ottoman Empire. No one heeded to their cries and poverty. Why would they keep the records of the names of the visitors? What were the odds of anyone finding the trace of the existence of Shlomo Molcho's wife in Tsfat? According to the legend, his child was born somewhere else. After she heard the story about the man offering help, Aviva said with a smile:

'Everyone here can read your mind. People living in Israel are insightful and excellent soul searchers. Many understand what you have under your tongue even before you look for words there.'

He was uncertain whether her comment should be taken seriously. They were making plans for Shabbat, and she mentioned her friend living just off Art Colony that invited both for dinner. They had plenty of time until then and embarked on another adventure; Aviva wanted to show him where to look for the list of the burials in the cemetery during the Ottoman rule. That was the only source he could rely on to find any trace of the people who were connected to Shlomo Molcho. They enjoyed the walk and each other's company until it was time to go to Aviva's friend.

The rain never reaches these hills in June. Soil hardens, absorbs all moisture, and keeps it locked in the roots deep in the ground. The winds may move air back and forth above and around the town and even spread the parchment of clouds, but the drops of rain are unknown. Yet, Gabriel is dreaming of warm summer raindrops bouncing off his face, crawling down his chest through the unbuttoned shirt and swirling in his mouth. He woke up at the darkest hour of the night, feverish and feeling that his tongue turned into a dry stripe of leather. Friday night in Tsfat is quiet, solemn, full of dreams. The time when prayers offered at the opening of Shabbat reach the Queen in her glory. Yet Gabriel was disturbed and burned with fever in the town where he knew no one. The words of the dream dreamed a long time ago echoed in his head at this dark hour while he was trying to fight off the nightmare. He was reduced to the aching ball of nerves:

'I do not understand. I was just trying to find which of the three ships is the one that would take me to the right destination. I did not want to solve any riddles. I do not want to be caught in the dreams of other people. This is not my dream.'

He finally understood what the mirage was trying to reveal. His mind grasped the message hidden for a long time in a remote corner of memories. Anxiety and uneasiness often spoiled his brief pleasures since the beginning of the journey. The feeling that he is losing the ground under his feet occasionally occurred since he made the first steps in the Land. He had the constant feeling of being an impostor within his own quest; not the one who draws plans and decides, but a vessel navigated from somewhere else. That distant power was the one that made choices and took turns on the road to an unknown destination. Finally, he could understand the purpose of his existence. He was a shell, a chalice created to hold dreams, longings, and sorrows of others. Someone or something was guiding him, sent strangers to offer help without being asked for it, and set him on a journey from one place to another in search of names, dates, and memories that connected them.

He took a long shower, and the fever subsided. After this, he could sleep through the rest of the night. On Sunday morning he called the number handed to him in the café on Ha Ari street four days before. Aviva had already left, and he could focus on solving the mystery of Yossi and his offer. The man invited him to meet at the same place as the first time. He entered the café exhausted by carrying a canvas bag full of books that made him pant and sweat for a few minutes. Gabriel did not show any compassion for Yossi's troubles and wanted his questions answered and fast.

'How did you know who I am, Yossi? How did you know what I was looking for in Safed?'

Yossi took out his phone and spent some time searching through its content, then turned the screen to Gabriel. He saw his picture. Couple of them. One from the passport, the other taken while he was in the hotel lobby in Tel-Aviv. Mystical reasons had nothing to do with their first meeting. He was followed. This was not unusual, and Gabriel reluctantly had to accept the fact that a stranger without contacts and relatives entering Israel for the first time would look suspicious. The search for his family history with no living relatives in Israel, travelling alone without a set itinerary, can all be the reason for being followed around by people like Yossi. He did not do this for money and really wanted to be of help to Gabriel. He studied at the local yeshiva, had a job and a family. Apparently, he knew a lot about the history of Tsfat and all lustrous residents it harboured over the centuries. Unfortunately, not much was left after a few major earthquakes in the area, and he could not show him the house where Rabbi Molcho sojourned in town. He could take him there or to Meron.

The story shifted to kabbalah and the meditations for summoning the angels. This was not the first time Gabriel heard stories about Molcho's communication with the maggid, an angel who would be compelled to advise the person who pronounced his name. He would be coerced to reveal the outcome of important events in the future, especially disasters that could be better controlled and not claim human lives. It was rumoured that Shlomo Molcho summoned one of these angels and helped ease the effects of the flood in Rome. He warned the Pope to leave the city. He also sent a message to John III, the king of Portugal, warning him of an imminent earthquake. The occurrence of a deadly flood on October 8th, 1530, and the earthquake in Lisbon on January 26th, 1531 happened, as predicted by Shlomo Molcho. Yossi did not mention these accomplishments with admiration. He said he would not break bread with people who engage in this kind of practice. He also made a stern face when the name of Clement VII was mentioned in the conversation. It was a useless waste of time on a lost cause. Jewish prayers, meditation, and learning were not supposed to be discussed in front of the undeserving. It is a mistake punishable by death.

Molcho lived when Jewish religious courts would not act on matters pertaining to practical kabbalah. The elders of the communities that spurred transgressors delivered them into the hands of celestial powers for judgement. A person who taught the Torah to the undeserving brought upon his head the punishment from the higher realms, not angry community members. Gabriel was shocked by the last sentence that stated that Shlomo Molcho deserved the punishment of death at the stake. Yossi refused to take a forgiving attitude to his progenitor. No one uses the keys of the chambers that are made only for the few and live. Had it not been the Inquisition, he would have fallen into the hands of robbers, or wild animals, or die in another way; yet we should accept the fact that using the forbidden names, engaging in forbidden meditations, would bring the person to a complete ruin. Of course, the blow never comes immediately. The punishment does not follow the transgression at once. Sometimes it takes months, even years, for the judgement to be executed. Rabbi Molcho died because he used forbidden knowledge. Even though earned the protection of Clement VII, ultimately, he had to perish. Did Molcho expect the Pope to protect him from the rage of heaven? Molcho brought all this upon himself.

The Letters on the Box

He paused and stared at the wall. Maybe he was contemplating whether to continue the conversation on the topic or was trying to gather his thoughts and articulate them more effectively. The discourse was going deeper into tackling the facts of the realm of mysticism, and Gabriel was not particularly inclined to converse on Kabbalah with Yossi. The term has been misused and profaned in recent decades; no one took it seriously except for those who were studying it or studying about it.

Later that night, he opened the book that he just purchased. It was an introduction to the concepts of Jewish mysticism by Rabbi Aryeh Kaplan, titled 'Meditation and Kabbalah', work attractive enough to appeal to the ordinary reader. It is a valuable source of information on the topic to anyone who could not read and understand Hebrew. Aviva told him to get the book after he shared his dreams about the woman, the ships, and the golden box. The latter was a secret he told no one before. Gabriel thought of dreams as more intimate than any events during wake hours. Sharing one's dreams is as personal as any cause of infirmity. Nightmares are the ailments in need of treatment and cure; they may be the reason to see the doctor as any physical ailment and pain; Gabriel expected no one to unfold his thoughts and help him understand the messages sent from the dark side of his mind.

It was a strange feeling–sharing the memory of a dream; an attempt to decode feelings and concepts that may not be comprehensible to anyone, least of all the dreamer. The only tool at his disposal was speech, and once enclosed in words, the entire construct collapsed. Human language is a communication tool employed with little success. To his own surprise, Gabriel was comfortable sharing his dreams with Aviva. Even the one, the most secret of all.

He just turned thirteen before a trip with his family to a skiing resort in the mountains. The hotel was at the foot of the ski slope, on the very narrow plateau cut in the rocks. They arrived at the closing of the day and the first view of the scenery was one of sparkling whiteness of the snow illuminated by the rising moon. The beauty of the moment has burrowed a hole in his soul and filled it with unspeakable longing. He was standing by the window of the hotel room, gazing at the smooth ice-clad side of the mountain covered in silver light. When he fell asleep, he had the dream of a woman, more of a ghost of a woman than the living being. She appeared as a translucent silhouette, and her eyes were devoid of light. The appearance filled the room with a hostile presence. Although the facial features of the apparition were soft and youthful, they did not reflect any emotion and filled him with fear. Feeling threatened by the presence, he tried to wake up. The vision was moving about the room, seemingly indifferent to his presence. She occupied the space above and around. When he shifted slightly in place, the ghost turned in his direction and stared with empty eyes and a stern face. Then she opened her hand, and he saw something on the outstretched palm. The hand had two thumbs, one on each side. A tiny golden box was in the middle. After he conquered fear, still asleep, he tried to take a better look at the box–it was the fine piece of solid gold with tiny letters etched on all sides, inside and out. He could not make out what they spelled. He recognized individual letters but failed in any attempt to read the text. He was staring at the inscription, eyes transfixed on the box, until his vision got too blurry to see anything.

The letters were jumping off the surface and around him; a ghostly woman caught them with the thumbs of her hands and stuffed them into her mouth. When no letters were left, she clapped, and exclaimed:

'How many letters have I swallowed?'

Then she engaged in swirling and dancing, pouncing, and jumping around the terrified boy, and the letters flew like sparks of light. Gabriel tried to make out what they were one more time and failed again. The apparition obviously read his mind, because it bounced off the ceiling and whispered into his ear:

'Would you like to know my name?'

'Yes,' muttered, frightened to death, thirteen-year-old Gabriel Marcus. However, the vision disappeared into the cold winter night, and he woke up with the feeling of heaviness in the chest. He did not go skiing the next morning or any other while on the mountain and spent the rest of the family vacation in the hotel room fighting high fever and other symptoms attributed to the sudden onset of a flu. Gabriel knew it was not the flu he suffered from. He touched the boundaries of the other side, the realm of husks and spiritual impurity. His soul was poisoned by the vision in the dream. Gabriel never shared this with anyone and tried to push it deep into the secret garden where other nightmares and sorrows of his childhood lived. The first time he saw the tiny silver box from his mother's rag doll, he shook with terror as the images of the ghost and its golden twin emerged behind the wall of painful memories. It lasted only a moment. Then he looked carefully at the surface with the flag and the inscription in Hebrew. The letters did not fly away or dance around the room. It looked different, oval, not a cube. Yet the owner of the silver box with the flag and the golden box in a dream was the same person. He will learn this only many years later.

Rabbi Chaim Vital wrote: *'There are four universes: Atzilut, Beriyah, Yetzira and Asiyah... While the Temple was standing the Prophets could see into the universe of Atzilut, though it was clothed into the light of Beriyah... When the first Temple was destroyed, this was not possible, and the lights from the universe of Atzilut and Beriyah were not revealed at all. This is the meaning of the teaching that after Hagai, Zechariah, and Malachi, prophecy ended completely, and only Ruach HaKodesh remained. This Ruach HaKodesh comprises the transmission of the lights of the universe of Yetzirah, but the lower level as well... There are given techniques through which one can open the gates of the physical world to enter Asiyah and Yetzirah... and these practices were used by Rabbi Akiva and the members of the Great Assembly. These techniques were then forgotten. Besides this, the ashes of the Red Heifer were lost in the period of the later Talmudic sages... during the generation of Abaya and Rava who lived in the fifth century. From then on, people only made use of techniques involving the universe of Asiyah. Since this is the lowest of the universes, its angels have only a little good and are mostly evil. Besides, this is a level where good, and evil are closely intertwined. This does not bring any enlightenment since it is impossible to perceive good alone and one's perception is, therefore, a combination of good, and evil, truth, and falsehood.*

It is forbidden to make use of these techniques since evil attaches itself to the good. One may intend to cleanse his soul, but because of the evil, he defiles it. Even if one gains some perception, it is truth intermingled with falsehood. This is especially true today since the ashes of the Red Heifer no longer exist. The uncleanliness of the husks attaches itself to the individual who attempts to gain enlightenment through summoning the angels with incantations of their names. This is known as practical Kabbala. Therefore, he who watches his soul should keep far from it… We have a tradition that an individual who is not careful in this matter and still uses the meditations to summon the angels will be punished in this world. Either he or his children will become sick, will be impoverished, or will become apostates. Learn a lesson from Joseph Della Reina and Rabbi Shlomo Molcho, who made use of the practical Kabbala and were destroyed from the world. All this is because of the above reason. This involves a realm where there is no good devoid of evil. Besides this, it involves coercing angels with oaths against their will. These angels retaliate by enticing this individual, drawing him into evil ways until his soul is destroyed. Beyond this, the methods involving these oaths were concealed by earlier generations revealed only to the few, and we are not well-versed in the proper techniques. One must therefore keep himself far from these things.'

Gabriel closed the book at this point and spent the rest of the day thinking about choices he made and decisions that envisioned this journey; He created the list of actions that were leading to this moment with the hotel room in Tsfat, Israel, reading the book where his martyred ancestor is mentioned. The decisions Shlomo Molcho made that had him burnt at the stake. He thought about his grandfather who died in Auschwitz and others between the two who existed in the past four centuries. Any object, any word that testified to their existence was touched by the realms beyond tangible reality. They all lived under the same curse, dangerously close to the other side. Gabriel had to search for answers in the universe where his ancestors dwell, free from pain, blessed with a perfect understanding of the reasons for their suffering. Gabriel finished the bottle of wine Aviva left for him in the room. He sank into the warm, silent night with no dreams.

Tapestry

Anna P. did not believe in soulmates. She thought people should eat the sack of salt together to grow close. Once they get through it, they could claim the knowledge of each other's soul. They may share the music they hear in dreams and leave the messages made of pebbles and seashells that only two of them can understand. To believe in a soulmate, you must be the one of few that had the encounter with the androgynous self. If you shared this experience, you would spend the rest of your days on earth basking in the rare blessing granted by heaven. If you had this experience but could not be reunited with your twin soul, you may spend the rest of your life contemplating insignificant occurrences. e.g., how the number of knots turns into tapestry hanging on the walls in the museum; how much time it would take to turn tiny silk threads of different colours and hues into the portrait of a woman. The woman dressed in a velvet gown with folds in the colour of sage and olive branches. Her hair covered with a veil and her eyes turned inward, away from the visible world. They appear closed if the tapestry is approached from the left. Yet, watching from the right, the eyes would stare straight at the onlooker and the face would reflect the subtle shine of golden threads embroidered in the design. Anna P. explored the details that made this face exquisitely expressive. It appeared alive in the silk design. Still, she could not name the emotion saved in the portrait. It made her inquire about the living person who inspired the craft work of perfection. What about the life beyond motionless memory that survived the challenge of time and moved hands that tied the knots? Anna P. wondered if the art and skill of the artist did the service to the living by this depiction in silk and gold. The person who inspired the artist was long forgotten. The plaque next to the portrait spelled the name of Vittoria Colonna. There was nothing else, and Anna had to look her up after the visit to the museum. A woman whose image was embroidered in silk and hung in the museum, far from her original home, mattered no more. People did not come to admire the life that inspired, but the skill, effort, and talent that made soft folds in the hue of sage and olive colours, or cream silk veil hiding the eyes that could look at the visitors under the closed lids. No one cared about life beyond inspiration.

When she returned home after a month spent in Britain, Anna P. took upon herself to learn more about the poet whose portrait echoed sadness that was impossible to forget. The marchioness, the muse, a friend of many talented artists of the generation, was the epitome of longing, sorrow, and solitude. Anna P. imagined Vittoria as a fairy that had a gift to wrap her sad feelings into the leaves of the trees that could sing when pressed against the lips and placed her tears under the pebbles on the shore of Tyrrhenum Sea. She had dark holes in the soul, just like Anna P. They were the same kind: those who do not feel at home in this world and walk with an abyss in their souls. They dream but do not understand the dreams; They are always on a quest, looking for love only never to find it, willing to sacrifice their lives for the sake of leaving the loneliness behind, yet unable to shake it off even in death.

Anna P. did not believe in soulmates. They were only the involuntary collisions on the highway running through eternity. Even worse, they were an attack on personal integrity; a tide of powerful emotions, followed by ebbing and dull stagnation. This was the most favourable definition of the romantic relationship she could think of.

Even if it lasts a lifetime, it is impossible to fill the void. Romance cannot etch the permanent and meaningful line in a soul.

She did not consider herself a cynical misandrist. Besides, in time she learned to hide her inner self, as she called it, in contrast to whatever she would expose to the world. Neither was she a hypocrite, nor an actress. No one would understand. She kept her secret; that was the best course of action; kept her safe; protected people who took part in her life. When she needed to comfort herself, she wrote poems. They were long, composed without rhyme, and full of sadness. The poems had the form of the letters written to a lover that she never met, gentle odes to the winds that have taken her away from the source of light, nourishing hope, and kindness. Her poetic epistles were deceptive to the reader; the genuine despair they expressed was not. She shared none of this with anyone. Anna P. did not believe in soulmates.

She recognised different pathways taking her to all outcomes of her decisions and discerned the time any outcome would give her. That is how she knew all roads ahead got to a place where they tie into a knot. Whichever way she turned, there were walls. All roads she took came to an abrupt stop. Her life will end in a particular spot at a certain moment. She will die young. Each step would bring her closer to the end of the road. Somehow, Ana knew she would die in a traffic accident, run over by a drunk driver who suddenly sobered up from the previous night filled with cheap liquor and fighting his wife, who threatened to leave him. This time for good. She could have died on another day, not on that morning, but everything else would have been the same.

Gabriel went through all stages of grieving after the fatal accident. For many weeks after the funeral, he traced her route from home to the spot on the road where she was hit, pacing each of his steps to resemble the way she would walk and do whatever she did. He was trying to think of that moment; the mind occupied with a thought of worry or anything that distracted her from watching the road and being more careful. Then he stopped and sank into quiet mourning. He left his room only to take a bite of food. He stopped talking to all his friends. This went on for weeks until he received the box with Anna's poetic journals, notes, and letters. The poems and notes he found inside shifted his grief to astonishment. Her poetic aspirations, sombre splendour of the verses, hushed yet ever-present inclination to go deep inside and rummage about the memories of other people's dreams was Anna he did not know. He did not recognise her at all. It was as if he only discovered the actual person hidden in the body of someone he had dated for a few years. That other person did not love him, did not long for his presence, did not mourn over a lost opportunity for spending more time together. He felt betrayed on a different level–one that involves longing for the soul dwelling in a different place, not the one where we toil our time.

When he started the quest into the elusive past of his ancestors, he remembered the name of Vittoria Colonna. He remembered the tapestry that made Anna return a few times to gaze at the portrait during her visit to the heritage house in Somerset, England. He read the note again, but except for the vivid and detailed description of the exhibit and the footnote on the biography of the poetess, there was no other mention of the name. The discovery of the note on Vittoria Colonna astonished him. He did not consider it a coincidence.

As he was going deeper into learning about the times and death of Solomon Molcho, he stopped believing in coincidence. There were too many events with an obvious impact on the direction his life took. He could not explain them as random occurrences.

PART THREE

Alacrity and Alertness

Gabriel Marcus described the visit to Tsfat as a ground-breaking experience. It was so not for the wisdom that grew out of it, neither the specific circumstances, nor the people he met, but the change it brought from within. Whatever took place in Tsfat stirred his sails in a different direction. From then on, he had his eyes wide open and looked at the world differently. His views were focused on alacrity and alertness.

'Wake up from slumber. It is time,' said his father in the morning on weekdays. Every morning he would pull the drapes ajar and yell to get him to wake up and get ready for school. Alacrity and alertness are needed to understand the purpose of one's existence. He was not alarmed by his nightmares anymore. He learned how they crossed over to reality. The visit to Tsfat changed everything.

None of the characters that took a place on the stage of a short, intense life of Diogo Pires, named Solomon Molcho later in life, deserved more resentment than the holy Roman Emperor, Charles V. He was the eldest son of Philip the Handsome of the Austrian House of Habsburg and Joanna the Mad of the Spanish House of Trastamara (daughter of Ferdinand of Aragon and Isabella of Castile). Holy Emperor was a child born from parents who suffered the consequences of inbreeding. They were predisposed to many ailments and conditions invested in them by corrupted genetic material. In addition, Charles V was a man with no shame. He courted several mistresses simultaneously, his step-grandmother among them. He went through a few broken engagements and finally married his first cousin. His mother Joanna was suffering from insanity. She may not have been insane, but politics required that she should be removed from the position of power. He kept her, his own mother, imprisoned until her death and ruled instead. The king was full of disdain for her. Alas, it was her lineage and not his father's that earned him the right to the throne. The diet throughout Charles's life was predominately based on red meat, which consequently caused severe issues with gout. The condition deteriorated until he could not walk anymore and had to resign from any public affairs for two years before his death in 1558. Holy in the name, preserved and repeated over centuries, sounds like a sarcastic reference to this biography.

Charles V met with Shlomo Molcho in 1532 at the request of the latter and his companion David Reubeni. The meeting was requested in the hope to inspire the mighty ruler for a war against Muslim Turks and the Ottoman Empire. The exact course of the conversation is not known, but the audience with the throne certainly went awry as Molcho and Reubeni were imprisoned by the Inquisition. This occurred at the request of Charles V, who claimed the duet should be put on trial for heresy. The encounter with Molcho and Reubeni was two hours long, and it was not the first time the king enjoyed the company of rabbi Molcho. Therefore, it was not clear what made him change his previous attitude of respect and some admiration for an adamant decision to send both men to the gallows. Sometimes later, when Solomon Molcho was charged by the court in Mantua, the king offered the pardon if the accused would promise to return to being Diogo Pires, not Shlomo Molcho, but the offer was rejected. It must have amused the fornicator and the glutton of a king to make such an offer, knowing it would never be accepted; throw the promise of life for a soul. This episode, however, cannot be retold with the complete accuracy unless the travel companion, teacher, and role model of Shlomo Molcho - David Reubeni - is properly introduced and his role in the events over the years, ending in tragic death sentence for both, explained.

David Reubeni was a Jewish political activist. The mysteries of Reubeni's origins are stories told to the present days. His origin and intentions have been stipulated by many, but never fully understood. Gedaliah Ibn Yahya speaks of him as a man of dark complexion and of low stature. His place of origin, as well as the year of his birth and death, remain unknown. In 1525, he secured the audience with the King John of Portugal on the recommendation of Pope Clement VII.

Reubeni claimed he was of noble origin and born in 1490 in the harbour of Khaybar, which is identified with a place of a similar name in central Arabia. When he was in the audience with king John of Portugal, he spoke only Hebrew and Arabic and required a translator. During the visit, he claimed he was sent by his brother, the king of Khaybar, by the name of Joseph, who ruled the kingdom with seventy elders and was seeking alliances against the Ottoman Turks. Military forces were to be employed against the Turks who conquered the area for its great wealth. In another version, his origin was traced to a port called Cranganore, on the Malabar Coast of India, where a large and vibrant Jewish community had lived for many centuries. The historians place Reubeni's origin in Afghanistan.

Daoud Roubeni is the name of a legendary hero of the Pushtun tribes. The historians claim that a large Jewish community lived in Firuzkuh, the lost capital of Afghanistan. David Reubeni may have come from this area. There is little evidence for this theory beyond Jewish presence in the country.

Scholars are also reluctant to believe in Reubeni's claims to nobility, even though he insisted he was the son of a deceased monarch. He said he held the ministerial position in the kingdom's war department while the country was ruled by his elder brother. This kingdom had three hundred thousand Israelite subjects.

At other times, he said he descended from the tribe of Judah. The tree of lineage traced his ancestry back to king David. Regardless of the disagreements about the family tree, there is some evidence that he was of Sephardi origin and lived in Israel. He possessed the excellent knowledge of the Land, especially the holy places. It also seems that he was connected to the sages of Jerusalem. There is one Torah scholar mentioned in connection to David Reubeni: a famous rabbi and cabbalist Avraham ben Eliezer Halevi. Expelled from Spain, Halevi took refuge in Portugal, but was forced to convert with all other members of the community. In 1506, he left Portugal for Italy. Then he embarked on travel through Greece and Egypt. He finally settled in Jerusalem under the Ottoman rule. He calculated and wrote about the date of the redemption. He provided messianic interpretations of the contemporary events: Ottoman conquests, the rise of Martin Luther, and the growing interest of Christian scholars in Jewish scripture and literature. His works generated interest in Europe, particularly Italy, which explains the initial success of David Reubeni's plans and proposals. When Reubeni landed in Venice in 1523, wealthy members of the Jewish community subsidised him, paid the debts incurred during his trip. They provided the references for the audiences with influential members of the clerical circles.

Dressed in a turban, striped silk and covering most of his short body with the white scarf, he wondered around the courts of noblemen, wealthy conversos and cardinals all the way to meeting with king John III of Portugal where he demanded the donation of a warship and the joint military action to free the Christian nations and the Land of Israel and push the Ottoman Turks back into Asia Minor.

Shlomo Molcho was employed as a scribe at the king's court at the time and was deeply moved by the exotic traveller. He was not the only one. The community of conversos was trembling with inspiration, faith, and a hope Reubeni brought with him. There was not a single soul that did not look up to him and rejoiced in redemption from terrible suffering that had befallen Jewish communities in this part of the world over the century time. Diogo Pires asked David Reubeni to teach him Torah. The latter, however, did not want to spend time with Diogo Pires and did not want to teach Torah to an uncircumcised Jew. At that point, Diogo Pires circumcised himself. He almost bled to death. Diogo Pires became Shlomo Molcho and publicised his heresy to the new Christians.

In all events that are mentioned in the previous discourse, there is little room for speculation. David Reubeni, whoever he was, had stirred the destitute, oppressed, and frightened souls of the communities in Italy, Spain, and Portugal, recalled the vision of Jerusalem and its glorious past, and lifted the hearts of the oppressed from darkness. From the time they started the journey together, the two had to travel separately and hid the fact that Shlomo Molcho was born and baptised Diogo Pires. Baptised Jews that returned to their faith were put on trial as heretics and usually sentenced to death by the Inquisition. The world around them had become a chess field, and they hoped to stay in the game for the longest time possible. The idea of Christian-Judeo war against the Ottomans and Islam has generated some interest but little genuine support. After the first visit to John III of Portugal, David Reubeni was thrown in prison for preaching Judaism to conversos. He was released from prison only on request from French king Francis I and with ransom paid by the Jewish community.

Charismatic Leaders

Aviva looked through the window in the morning and whispered:

'We do not need yet another charismatic leader.' The news was bleak, and all focused on the latest political crisis and its protagonists.

Gabriel emailed about his thoughts on the history of David Reubeni. He could not ignore his role in the rising and downfall of his ancestor. Two days ago, she read a paper on Shabtai Tzvi in an attempt to decode the inscriptions on the tombstones in the Jewish cemetery on Crete. Since the destruction of the second Temple, the world has had a fair share of the gifted candidates for national leadership. Jewish history pushed them onto the stage at the heights of the heat; Bar Kokhba, David Reubeni, Shabtai Tzvi, Jacob Frank; some of them have paved road to eternity with dead bodies of their followers. All of them were witnesses to the devastation and despair.

This is true. They all came out of the darkest of nights for Jews: Roman persecution after the destruction of the second Temple and expulsion from Jerusalem inspired famous Rabbi Akiva to appoint Bar Kokhba the leader of the nation; David Reubeni struggled to find a home for the people after the expulsion from Spain; Shabtai Tzvi and Jacob Frank misled many with their madness after Khmelnitsky pogroms. There seems to be a list of misfortunes and horrors in every century that opened the mind of the people to blind trust in miracles, as nothing short of miracles could help them deal with cruelty, injustice, and hate of the world. None of these false messiahs came and claimed the role of the redeemer out of low, mundane reasons. They were all witnesses and victims of unbearable suffering that took place over several generations. They all felt invited to do their share of redemption. Life in the diaspora had become impossible for many. They could only cleave to pure faith and hope their cries would be heard. The ultimate redeemer would bring all troubles to an end. Those episodes ended in disappointment. Yet the failed expectations were followed by harbingers of change. They gave rise to those who carried the pennant with more success; after David Reubeni came Rabbi Luria, Shabbatai Tzvi was followed by Baal Shem Tov. The Holocaust has caused the efforts to shift from search for the redeemer to building the place of redemption. The people understood the importance of the return to the land of Israel. The hope of reaching Jerusalem in heaven wisely started with the work on the ground. When the modern state of Israel was established and announced, no one was looking for charismatic individuals to fill the role of the Messiah. Millions of miracle workers were in demand; the circumstances called for the miracle to build the country from nothing. A tremendous amount of faith, love and perseverance were needed to turn the desert sand into fertile land and survive amidst the packs of hungry wolves.

Pogroms and expulsions, murders and devastation triggered dispersion across the globe. They also caused the return to the land in modern times. They contributed to the collective wisdom and unity seldom shared by other nations. Millions died but we still claim what had been given to our forefathers millenniums before. Aviva understood the inspiration of David Reubeni and Shlomo Molcho. She understood the circumstances that spruced it up. She learned about the mistakes that caused their tragic end. Those who stand on the hill see both the valley and the distant horizons. They see the storm clouds rolling ahead of those dwelling on lower grounds. Unfortunately, both the dwellers of the valley, and those on the mountain peaks, underestimated the power of ignorance, greed and, above all, true intentions of self-proclaimed keepers of the truth.

While they were away from home, Jews built communities established on the values cherished since the beginning of time. They supported Torah scholars, who spread love for learning and passed it on to the next generation. 'From generation to generation' has become the mantra of Judaism, even if it meant sacrifice and suffering. The tight-knit communities stood by their charismatic leaders but could not always prevent their demise. If they were thought to be the enemies of any established religious or political order, they would be persecuted and murdered by authorities of the gentiles.

The charismatic leaders came with the flaw. They seldom understood the gentiles did not share the idea of faith so dear to Torah scholars. It had to mature and age to be shared. Most often, non-Jews worshipped, observed, and approached the divine only after afflicting it with human attributes; they preached a religion of love, yet spread death everywhere; yelled from the pulpits about simplicity and poverty while amassing wealth; advocated for altruism and viciously fought for power; cried for compassion, peace and unity and murdered anyone who attempted to change the order of their affairs.

Kuzari

Anna P. believed people were born into their families and lived in their homes in places, in countries that occupied different spots on the map of the world. This would be the outward identity. More important was the hidden identity. The secret of hidden identity was revealed only to the few. That implied that most people never discovered who they were. Some had the hint but did not bother to understand. Some denied what they found and tried to hide it with cunning diversions. People who recognised and understood their true self were usually those who knew how to use it: owning one's full potential meant owning the world. Anna had her list of the hidden identities of nations and ethnicities that cannot be found in the school history books. She played a game of search for 'who really are the people she had met.'

In her genealogy or genography, most people were Khazars. She recognized them by the colours of their dreams and the taste of salt on their skin. Anna would observe the way a person moved the thumb or pressed heel in the sand and say how many lifetimes that soul was around. She believed that people who worshiped winds of the seas and sang the mermaids to sleep would sail the world and never felt at home when their shoes were at the doorstep. She judged people by the size of their bite and the echo of their laughter that stayed in the room after they had left.

'Souls were created at the beginning of time. There are a few souls inhabiting the world. They were shattered into pieces, changed the bodies, emerged under different names and different parts of Earth, yet they did not change and did not lose the names given to them at the moment of creation. Their journey from one body to the next will continue until the end of time. When the time comes, they will be summoned to take the original shape and place they were given by the Creator. They will praise the Throne of Glory.' (written and dated two years prior to Anna's death)

She supported her beliefs with historic facts and according to those Kuzaris had likely moved to many countries once their kingdom had been destroyed; It is neither a miracle nor a legend that people are born with their souls all around the world. I asked if she knew anything about Jewish souls scattered around the globe when I started the search for the descendants of Shlomo Molcho.

I also wanted to know if this genealogy would recognize there were people comfortable with the soul they were given and would not change it for anything in the world. Apparently, the hidden identity of our souls would be the major reason for all kinds of ailments and issues impossible to resolve during one lifetime.

'What would you be, Anna? Where does your soul place you in the grid of soul identities?'

'I do not know. My dreams belong to someone else. I dream of an island with green rocks, steep cliffs rising from the sea waves. I walk on the shore that is covered in sand lilies and drink bitter wine.'

'I still do not know where your soul came from, only that you dwell in a beautiful place in your sleep.'

Anna smiled and promised to take me to one of her walks on the green island in her dream.

Gabriel remembered his dead girlfriend in the sultry afternoon hours on the last day of his visit to Tsfat. As he dozed off, it was uncertain whether she emerged from his thoughts while asleep. Yet, the gentle flow of breeze coming through the cracks in the blinds made him remember her.

The memories did not bring pain with them. 'It happened many years, 'he whispered to the wind. The knot in his stomach did not tighten when he thought of her as many times before. Her youthful presence was still vivid, so beautiful. The voice, abundant and warm, echoed in his mind. To end the episode of daydreaming, Gabriel jumped to his feet with unexpected vigour and packed the bags to be taken to the car. He wanted to get going before dark and leave shadows behind. He did not want to take any of that back to Tel-Aviv.

Rosh Hashanah 1280

Aviva waited for him at a restaurant on King George Avenue, kissed him on the lips upon arrival and asked about two days he spent on his own. Her routine had been just as usual. She wanted to share thoughts on David Reubeni and what she learned from the reviews of his journals and the community chronicles. There was some greatness in him, but he was not cut for a leader. His charisma, expertise and manipulative skills were exhausted within a two-hour conversation with Charles V. The stories of noble lineage, mysticism, holy mission all faded before the unholy 'holy' king. The suffering of David Reubeni was worse than what Shlomo Molcho had to endure. The story of his adventures and demise support everything said earlier: our people do not need charismatic leaders. Charisma wears out quickly and turns into dust under the feet of the seasoned politicians and cruel rulers. David Reubeni spent many years in prison, and the date of his demise is not recorded with certainty. According to some, he was poisoned by the Spanish Inquisition between 1535 and 1541. Another record states he was burnt at the stake in 1541.

Benvenida Abravanel, the wife of Samuel Abravanel, the prominent member of the community in Italy, had a silk banner embroidered with Ten Commandments for David Reubeni. He carried it with him everywhere. Many crypto Jews reached out to show their respect and support; he was given money, shelter, protection, and recommendations that opened the doors of the gentile nobility. However, the journals left after David Reubeni reveal a different side of the charismatic adventurer altogether. The narrative revolves around the money he collected for the nonexistent cause and the enthusiasm of the Jewish community for the stories of the exotic traveller. The admiration diminished and ultimately disappeared in wake of the audience with the king. His community could not protect him once he broke the rules too many times and got blacklisted in courts throughout Portugal, Spain, and Italy. It was not possible to ransom Reubeni imprisoned on the account of forgery. The letters that guaranteed his mandate and identity were fake. Forgery was the last on the list of accusations adhering to his name. The change in perception of the community preceded the tragic ending. At the trial by the Inquisition, he was labelled an impostor.

The testimonies that remain behind him, journals (at least those that are authentic) do not offer more clarity on the intentions, goals, and identity of the short, stout. and eccentric Reubeni. Yet, the power of his faith cannot be denied. The hint at redemption given during public trials was genuine. He helped others understand the moment in history; the significant challenges put before communities in Mediterranean countries and pointed at resolution in the future. Unfortunately for him and the Jewish community, few understood the message. The same force that was leading him from one adventure to another and imbued him with the ability to raise hope, empowered his enemies with fierce anger and resolution to hunt him down. Those are the circumstances that brought David Reubeni and Shlomo Molcho to their tragic end.

'It is difficult to inspire people to do any good for others. This trait becomes especially prominent in times of calamities. I do not understand how Reubeni and Molcho got to suggest a crusade against Ottoman Empire. What made them think Charles V could start a war to free the Christian heretics and Jews?' -continued Aviva.

'The answer is: Abraham Abulafia. They were not the first in line to fight the impossible battles. The great

Rabbi Abulafia also wanted to change history. He set on the journey to convert the Pope to Judaism. In 1280 he announced he would travel to Pope's residence and persuade him, Pope Nicholas III, to convert to Judaism on the day before Rosh Hashana. His intentions were announced far and wide, and when the Pope who lived in Suriano heard of it, he issued the order for Abulafia's arrest and death sentence. The death, of course, was by burning at the stake. Abulafia headed to Suriano. The stake was already erected to prepare for his arrival and the public trial. When he arrived, he found out that the Pope had died of an apoplectic stroke during the night.

Victorious and filled with a passion for the quest, he headed to Rome. At once, upon arrival, he was thrown into prison by the order of Friars Minor but was freed after a four-week detention. Why do you think they freed him? They were afraid of him. The Inquisition was afraid of Molcho too, and they had the rope placed tight around his neck while walking him to the auto-da-fe. They did this, so he would not pronounce cabbalistic formulas while walking to his death. The rope was set so tight that he could hardly breathe. It was briefly released to offer him to repent and go back to Christian faith. After he refused, they burned him. They were afraid of his spirit, his speech, and his prayers. In that way the Inquisition acknowledged the superiority of Jewish faith yet still burnt Molcho at the stake. Isn't that ironic? And stupid? I am fascinated by this episode and many others like this. I am furious and laugh at the same time.'- Aviva stopped talking but took Gabriel's hand and squeezed it in her as if she tried to infuse him with the power she felt after expressing her thoughts on Great Rabbi Abulafia.

'Yes, we are so powerful that our murderers have to strangle us, cut our tongue, burn our books to prove that

111

their chanting, prayers, and books are genuine. '- echoed Gabriel.

They have spent more time than both originally intended in the diner on King George. It was almost midnight when Aviva handed him the cup of tea, which they sipped in silence on the sofa in her apartment. He spent the night with her. It was the first time he felt someone's body so close and so right next to him since Anna died.

Stacte

Uriel has gone through all plants that could hide behind the name Nataf. It was uncertain what it stood for, though the translation into Greek was more of a descriptive nature than the name of the specific plant; just like stacte stands for the oozing substance and is not in fact the name of the plant used as one ingredient in Ketoret. Further, it is described as the sap of the balsam tree. He made a list of different balsam trees native to Israel; of items on the list, the one that possessed all the properties required to make it valid was named kataf in the Talmud, and corresponded to Commiphora Kataf, Commiphora Myrrha Arabia Felix- in Latin. It was a tree used for extracting myrrh, the precious liquid. In the process used to prepare myrrh for Ketoret, the tree is bruised, then dissolved in oil of balanos and simmered over a low flame. The next step calls for the pouring of boiling water over it. The myrrh and oil would sink to the bottom like a deposit; and as soon as this has occurred, the mixture would be placed in a sieve to remove the remaining water and the sediment squeezed through the press.

The next candidate on the list, Balm of Gilead, or Styrax Benzoin, was identified as the tree known for its strong, sweet fragrance from sticky, resinous buds. The resin has a vanilla-like fragrance. It was most often found in the books about traditional medicine and included in compounds used to treat worms, wounds, and sepsis. The list of ailments that could be treated with Styrax Benzoin include arthritis, bronchitis, chapped skin, coughing.

Uriel tried to extract resin from both trees. It took him years to have gum-like substance shipped from the Middle East and paid for in gold. The merchant who traded rare and difficult to get by items around the globe claimed the merchandise was genuine and demanded hefty compensation for the content of the boxes wrapped in waxed paper. Uriel took it to Rabbi Pesach to confirm the resin was from the trees that were on the purchase order. He travelled all the way to Volos for this purpose. After the trip, he logged his findings into the journal used to complete the work on the ingredients of the Ketoret. What he did not write were the words that Rabbi Pesach who told him at the end of the visit:

'Uriel, pay attention to the words of Rabbi Nassan: As one would grind the incense another would say grind thoroughly, thoroughly grind. Because the sound is beneficial for the spices.'

The order of the offerings in Temple service had the power to cleanse and heal the soul. On account of this, Uriel concluded the ingredients used for compounding the incense were chosen for their pharmaceutical properties too. Over the years, he studied and collected information on this matter. He spent time and resources to learn. Anything related to the Temple service mattered to the finest minutia. Therefore, not only the plants but the location and harvest time were subject to scrutiny. The dishes and containers used for storage and preparation, proportion and the amount of all ingredients were strictly regulated by the laws of incense. The scriptures mention eleven rather than four, yet fifteen distinct ingredients were compounded into the formula.

As the compounding of the Ketoret ceased and knowledge of fifteen ingredients was lost, the recitation of the description of the incense service in the Temple began. It was common for the entire communities to read this prayer with special dedication and passion, especially in the times of the plague. The order of the incense offering is read, not said from the memory. Each word of this section in the prayer book is so significant that a crown could be placed over it. That is how Ketoret is valued in the text of the Zohar and with those who understand its spiritual benefits.

Uriel was less inclined to dive into the mystical meaning of the Hebrew text. He was a rational person attracted to the medicinal properties of the ingredients. He cherished moderate views on religious observance and was not zealous to judge those who thought differently. However, even moderately observant person had to be passionate about the Ketoret. The incense offering was the holiest part of the Temple service; one performed twice a day with unwavering certainty. Everything related to the incense was exacted to the smallest detail.

Uriel had genuine personal reason for this quest. His son developed a serious form of asthma soon after birth. It seemed nothing could keep the severity of the attacks at bay, and visits to the doctor's office became a weekly routine. They had no effect on the course or frequency of the attacks and everyone made the same recommendations and repeated the same advice: trips to the mountains, islands in winter, sedatives - asthma was often treated as the condition of the nervous heart. Uriel did not listen to the advice given by the doctors. He studied about Ketoret.

The Pharmacist

'There is a powder, tea or tincture,' his wife mentioned, 'sold by the pharmacist in another part of the town.'

She heard about it from their relatives who heard about someone whose children suffered from the same condition. It should be inhaled, not drunk. The room would fill with a pleasant fragrance and healing vapours. She could not remember if she heard the name of the medication and what the ingredients were. This is the moment that marks the beginning of his work. He was going to follow the pebbles thrown along the path and the first one was a small white fabric bag tied with a blue thread, handed to him by an elderly pharmacist with a story added to it:

'I do not know what it is, but Mrs. Mallah and Mrs. Errera order it regularly and say it helps with the cough and breathing.'

Uriel did not want to inquire about the ailments of Mrs. Mallah and Mrs. Errera but wanted to know who made the content of the white fabric bags. The next step of the query took him up the squeaky stairway of the building located just off the Agios Dimitrios and into the dwellings of an elderly woman. There was no plaque with the name on the door, but he was already told her name was Mrs. Molcho. She was a daughter of a late spice merchant and compounder; a little woman with a warm face, a smile spreading all the way to the lines on the forehead, and a sharp look in the eyes that took a measure of Uriel through a slit in the door before opening ajar to face him. She stood silently between the hallway and the apartment for a minute, then said:

'Come back in a week when I going to prepare the formula. Do not arrive before ten in the morning. I do not work during the hours of the stern judgement.'

Uriel did not utter a word. He said nothing. He did not express his thoughts in any other way.

He did what he was told and returned to the crumbling building in the day and the hour when he would help Mrs. Molcho with her work. His life purpose changed. From the moment he stepped into the room to learn about the herbs that help ease asthma attacks, he was not sure whether the events that unfolded were not just a dream that he could not leave on the dark side in the morning. Since he started learning about the incense with Mrs. Molcho, his steps softened, and his shadow faded. The lines on his face disappeared and his skin was enveloped in sweet fragrance. When he was in the room working on the compound, he had to put on a linen gown, make sure his pockets were free of any pins, coins and take his shoes off. Mrs. Molcho opened several wooden boxes with tiny wooden keys and pushed under his nose, the content of each asking him to inhale its fragrance. She insisted on breathing in and holding breath while counting to ten each time. There were four large boxes and two of them contained amber-like resin. The others were small.

'You will take stacte, onycha, galbanum and frankincense in equal amounts...'

The room was neither hot nor cold, and the sun was throwing its golden sparks through the cracks in the blinds. Air was full of hushed scouring of mice in the walls and buzzing of insects outside.

Patched Up Souls

'I was married before', said Aviva during breakfast the next morning.

'It did not last. When we got married, we were undergrad students and my husband dreamt of enjoying the warmth of home, the listening ear, and the promise of a better future. Once the studies ended, he pulled the anchors and sailed into a storm. He got a job somewhere in the mountains, did not want to talk about work, skipped trips home for the weekends and stopped coming altogether one day. You could say he vanished. Except that I knew his whereabouts, but that did not make any difference. I still do not know what he does. He did not want a listening ear and the warmth of home anymore. There were no arguments, no bitterness... just silence. I have not heard from him in five years and do not think that anyone has.'

'I was not married,' Gabriel said. Mentioning Anna in this conversation felt out of place. He wanted to leave stirred feelings in Tsfat. He paused and dulled his voice to sound indifferent:

'I have had a girlfriend for a few years. We had a great time together. One day, she died in a traffic accident. It was a terrible shock and took me a while to return to normal life. I kept myself busy with work and travel ever since. My mother died a few years back, and that is when I put together the family tree. The quest for the missing links in the project has brought me here.

While talking, he was playing with a fork and made holes into the slice of toast, spread jelly in the shape of a flower on the edge of the plate, and pushed the drops of butter into the empty coffee cup. Aviva was watching in amazement until they both started laughing.

The rest of the days they spent in the white city were carefree and light. They walked around and about, took pictures of the buildings inspired by the Bauhaus movement from the first half of the twentieth century. The couple explored the world cuisine in restaurants all over Tel-Aviv. They did not speak about the future, for they both knew it was bright. Gabriel had set the itinerary for the next few months, including the time he would spend in Tel-Aviv and Jerusalem. He was excited about the forthcoming meeting with the leader of the synagogue and the principal of the place of continuous learning (the best way to explain the meaning of the term yeshiva to a layperson) in the community of Biet-El. Close to the meeting, he was nervous about all the expectations of the unchartered road ahead. He agreed to meet at Rabbi's request early in the morning.

'Six o'clock. That is what he said. Apparently, that is the end of his day at the yeshiva as he learns during the night.'- he said to Aviva.

Aviva was familiar with the habits of the observant people from her years spent in Tsfat. She knew the schedule of the prayers may be one for everyone, but individual learning times differed. It was not at all unusual that Torah scholars learn in shifts for many hours of day and night. The head of the yeshiva was one of the leading religious authorities in the city; his request for unusual time of the meeting was not to be questioned. So, they headed together from Tel-Aviv to Jerusalem at the break of dawn and parted at the entrance of Mahane Yehuda Market, in the neighbourhood called Geula, after Aviva asked him to study the instructions to all street crossings and turns on the way to synagogue.

Once he reached the destination, he could not decide which entrance to choose and was certain that the decorative one made of bronze and posed as the only door to the old building was not in use. He stopped to admire its design and understand what it represented, when a young man poked his head through the adjacent window and asked if he could be of any help.

Gabriel did not speak Hebrew, but could use it to understand basic vocabulary and read. However, the man addressed him in English at once. Gabriel obviously could not have been mistaken for the native of the Land. The man let him in. He went through the barred metal gate and the double door before he got into the building. A clean, spacious, and well-lit foyer ended with the corridor which he took all the way to the last door in the raw of many. The man who admitted him entered the room first, then asked Gabriel to join him. Before leaving, he advised him to speak up because the Rav could not hear very well. The head of the yeshiva and the synagogue, Rabbi Yisroel Avichai, was a man of small stature, with a snow-white beard and sapphire blue eyes. He was sitting behind the massive desk, slanted forward in the velvet-covered chair and eyes focused on the recent visitor. He addressed Gabriel with a warm smile and said:

'Nu, where have you been for so long? Where have you been hiding?'

'It took me a long time to get here. It was quite a journey.'

'Your mother; you wrote about her and her passing. What did she die of?'

'Cancer. She was ill for many years, but the last onset of the disease did not take over two months; she died peacefully and experienced little pain.'

'Do you have any siblings?'

'No. I am the only child of my parents who are both deceased.

'Are you married? Do you have any children?'

'No, I am not, and I do not have any children.'

'Why are you here, Mr. Marcus?'

'I wanted to learn at the Yeshiva. I wanted to learn more about the cabbalistic meditations.'

This was not entirely true. The truthful answer would not fit into a single sentence, and he did not want to exceed the hospitality of the Rabbi and start a long soliloquy despite the initial arrangement of fifteen minutes of the time he was allotted when the meeting was scheduled.

'How old are you, Mr. Marcus?'

'Forty, soon to turn forty-one.'

'How much time are you willing to commit to learning?'

'As much as needed.'

'The need does not cease with your will. Sometimes it starts where the will would give up. Are you ready to go beyond your will to learn, Mr. Marcus?'

'I am.'

'Please, come back next Erev Shabbat at the same time.'

Just like that, the meeting was over, and he was led back into the street and could hear the locks been employed again and the metal gate closed. He walked to the old bronze door and continued to study the carvings and the inscriptions. The door had all seven gates leading into the old city of Jerusalem, the one above all others was sealed. He would visit all of them in the next two days.

Yossi in Jerusalem

As he was going through the Jaffa Gate into the busy crowd of tourists and locals, he thought he saw Yossi, his acquaintance from Tsfat, in front of one store at the very entrance into the shopping district. He tried to reach him but could not mingle through the group of people congregating around their guide, who obstructed the view and his attempts to take the side street where he thought he saw Yossi. After he completed the walk through three of the seven gates of the Old City, it was time for lunch, and he headed to the nearest patio to eat and rest.

A light tap on the shoulder and Gabriel almost choked on food in his mouth. He tried not to act annoyed when he turned to look at the intruder, who startled him during the meal. He forced a smile onto his face, and there he was, Yossi the guide, the nuisance, the spy (or something like that) with his ever-perplexed expression on the face, wrinkled white shirt, baggy black pants, and strings of the fringes of the tzitzits dangling down the hips.

'Gabriel, my friend, it is so nice to see you. How have you been?'

He reluctantly shared thoughts on his adventures and times between Tsfat and the present moment. He was tight-lipped about the short meeting on Rashi Street. While he tried to sound polite but not encourage further encounters with Yossi, he could not help but wonder whether Yossi already knew about his movements and daily trips. His sudden appearances over the past two weeks were unnerving. He was not indisposed by their interaction this time yet felt intimidated because Yossi persistently invaded his space. He kept coming back, despite Gabriel's obvious reservation about sharing anything related to his past and present life. He wanted to keep his matters private. Yossi understood the agreement that took place and did not press for more information. He wished Gabriel farewell and said:

'I am the good one. There are others interested in your whereabouts. You should be beware of them.'

With those words, he mingled into the crowd and disappeared, leaving Gabriel gaping after his last words, and wished he could have stopped him and ask for clarification.

496 out of 692

Uriel spent a few months learning about the formula that was used to compound the asthma medication, the only treatment that had success. His son was feeling better. Mrs. Molcho allowed him to assist with compounding and even mix the ingredients when his work entered the seventh month. During that time, he learned about three hundred different rules for mixing the herbs into the formula. He spent many hours studying and compiling the lists of possible and known species that were included in the incense formula. The extensive amount of work invested into his studies was crowned by improvement of his son's condition. At the break of the war, Uriel compiled the list of his discoveries: he had learned about 496 out of 692 species that are included in the family of Cassia. It is not clear why there are so many; he attributed brilliant success of the formula to spikenard of Nardus family. It is mentioned as a substance frequently used in perfumes, wine, and food. Pliny's Natural History lists twelve species of Nardus, including Lavandula Stoechas, and spikenard, Nardostachys Jatamansi. He saved enough money to purchase saffron, the most expensive spice in the world. It requires forty hours of labour to harvest 150.000 crocus flowers that render two pounds of spice. And those were only a few of the lots listed in the notes.

Uriel never used the same plants twice. Those were strict orders from Mrs. Molcho. She brought different ingredients for each batch they were preparing. Before including it in the formula, she would write and share the story of the origin of the specific plant. However, she never shared how she came into possession of the plants and spices. She would work on the formula for many days before sending it out to be sold.

Uriel never felt the need to ask how she learned the trade, or why it inspired lifelong dedication. He knew she had done it for decades; she prepared other concoctions used as remedies for different ails and pains and was known to healers throughout Northern Greece. She learned about herbs that heal from her father but compounding Ketoret was not shared in the family.

The notes that recorded many hours of study, information, and results of the extensive work on the formula were never discussed in her presence. She learned about Ketoret from the journals left behind after her father's passing. She never revealed the secret of his life's work to anyone. It was difficult to define what he was doing as his work was not given any name in his writings. Technically, he did not compound THE formula. Without the altar and the Temple, the priesthood, and the daily sacrifices, all things related to the service were nothing but an intellectual exercise that could not claim accuracy. The preparation of Ketoret for the needs of the Temple service prescribed the exact ingredients, proportions, and quantity. It was prepared annually, and whether the amount would be used during that time was determined by the size of the hands of the High Priest. It would happen that the surplus collected over sixty or seventy years could satisfy the needs for six months. Any manipulation with the process was liable to penalty and disqualified the product. However, the Temple was destroyed and the formula for the Ketoret lost. Mrs. Molcho's father, she, Uriel, as well as others who had a try at compounding, could not engage in sacrilege and their work had no connection to the Temple service.

Gabriel said nothing about meeting Yossi in Jerusalem. He mentioned the circumstances of their first meeting and shared only the content of their conversations in Tsfat.

He wondered whether the Jerusalem encounter should be discussed with Aviva or anyone else. The conversation had the tone of a warning, even a threat, or an overture to something even worse coming his way. Even though he could not stop thinking about it, he was not ready to express his fears and could not find the right words to discuss the incident. The last thing he wanted was to succumb to conspiracy theories and share them with anyone. Aviva came at the end of the week, on Thursday evening, and they rushed to enjoy the walk around the Old City a few minutes before sunset. She brought food for them from Tel-Aviv, so they planned to have the evening meal in Gabriel's hotel room.

He was quiet and reluctant to start the conversation about the events of the morning. He missed the opportunity to talk more about the encounter in Tsfat, which was understood more than a hoax, not a serious matter. After their meeting in the restaurant, the 'case of Yossi' required longer and unpleasant discussion on the matter that he found entirely unsuitable for the end of the working week. It would ruin the mood of the evening and the weekend with anxious stipulation over answers that could not be provided. Therefore, he postponed mentioning the meeting with Yossi in Jerusalem.

The Second Meeting

It is early in the morning, and Gabriel is on the road to Beit-El. He is less excited than last time. On that day, he expected the conversation about the admission to the house of learning. He considered it a formality after the first event. He was gravely mistaken. The same factotum let him in and took him to the same door as last time. He allowed Gabriel to enter the room alone and did not provide any further introduction. There were three men in the room sitting around the enormous desk that he noticed last time. Two of them were writing something and only glanced at him briefly, without greeting or addressing his presence in any other way.

The Rabbi, who conversed with him last time, greeted him, even attempted to stand up from his seat and offered Gabriel an empty chair in the middle of the room. He sat down, but did not feel comfortable anymore. That he was greeted only by one of the three people when he entered filled him with panic. He suddenly could not remember what he was going to ask and discuss on this occasion. After discomfort subsided, he kept silent and waited for the Rabbi or one of the other two men to start a conversation.

Soon a younger of the two lifted his eyes off the notebook and smiled encouragingly.

'My name is Avram Nissim. I and Rabbi Elfassi were asked by the Rosh Yeshiva to be here today and get to meet you. Did you have a hard time reaching Beit-El this morning?'

With that, he got up, poured himself tea, and offered a cup to Gabriel.

'Rosh Yeshiva wanted to discuss your plans and wishes regarding the study with our community in Jerusalem.'

Rosh Yeshiva said nothing except the initial greeting so far. He was staring at Gabriel and kept pulling his beard gently.

'We do not engage in learning about kabbalah if we are not well versed in all written and oral laws and have perfected the character traits. It is useless to engage in the study of the mystical concepts if one is not knowledgeable of the Torah laws and dedicated to living the Jewish life. Why are you not married, Mr. Marcus?'

The third man looked in his direction only when this question was asked. He was now staring at him, all focused on his face and waiting for the response.

Gabriel's confidence melted and disappeared between the bookshelves in the room. He heard his voice, but it sounded distant and strange.

'I was in a loving and meaningful relationship that could have transpired into a lasting companionship, but my girlfriend died in a traffic accident.'

'Was she Jewish?', this was the first time he heard the third man speaking and Gabriel was surprised by the sound of his voice. It was raspy, and he obviously found speaking difficult.

'No, she was not Jewish.', Gabriel responded quietly, while his voice turned into a whisper.

'Mr. Marcus,' Avram continued, 'what do you know about observances that fill the day of a Jewish man?'

Gabriel looked at the tip of his shoe and felt at the loss of words. What did he know about the daily observances of a Jewish man? He knew about the course of prayers, dietary restrictions, the names of the holidays, Shabbat... all this lived in him through the stories of his mother, books he read, brief meetings with religious people during his quests. Did this count as knowledge? A few fairy tales seen through the prism of his perception, a journey that could not bring him to the desired destination yet changed his life forever and took him deeper into memories of someone else that he can neither understand nor escape. No, he knew little about the daily observances of a Jewish man.

'We are all born under the premise that people have a choice. Jews do not have a choice. Once the yoke of the observance is taken, there is no way out of it. There is, but...', Rabbi Elffasi paused and shook his head.'

All this time Rabbi Avichai was gently pulling his beard and looking at Gabriel. His eyes were flames lit from within, and the expression on the face was compassionate.

'Gabriel,' he started in a soft voice, 'we are not trying to criticize you. What you have to think about is related to time; Jewish boys of our community commence learning at an early age; their parents, grandparents, and everyone else observe the laws of the day, the week, and the year. They do not start learning about kabbalah until they reach adulthood and get married. By then, they are already versed in the scriptures, philosophy and musar.'

He felt like an impostor, unsuitable and at odds like anywhere before and any other time in his life. Unable to fit, unable to find his place and belong; his dreams shattered multiple times, expectations ending in dire straits. He wanted to explain how much effort went into finding the place they were in; how much suffering preceded their meeting on that day but was at a loss for words and simply nodded his head and stood up to wish them farewell and leave.

Rabbi Avichai understood his intentions and told him: 'Come back next week before Shabbat. At the same time in the morning.'

The meeting has shaken him, and he wanted to share his impressions with Aviva. Instead, he started the conversation by talking about the encounter with Yossi.

It was not so much about Tsfat; what bothered him was that he saw him the day before in Jerusalem, and he did not even try to conceal it was not a coincidence. He did not want to stipulate on the warning, which might have been a ruse, and did not want to spawn conspiracy theories but could not stop thinking about the remark on the interest of someone, whoever that may be, into him and his visit to Israel.

Who was watching over his efforts to learn about the past of his family?

PART FOUR

Helping the Doves

He took on the private fast the first time he had the dream. However, it kept coming back. Every night he would see the doves in the courtyard. A flock of white birds, with tiny black dots for eyes, cooing softly around him until dark wings of falcons cast shadows from above. They tried to escape the claws of the predators, and he, Shlomo, waved his arms in despair. He tried to ward off birds of prey and protect the doves. He woke up in a cold sweat, startled; his heart beating wildly, disturbed by the dream. Fasting did not help, and he was advised to say the midnight prayer with each recurrence.

The hour was late; he was to be taken to his death early in the morning. Shlomo was not afraid, even though he knew his end would be a painful agony. He did not want to repeat the mistake of his parents. His soul would be reunited with the children of Jacob, not Esau. Death for the sake of the truth was a better choice than living with lies on the lips, serving the lie with hands and feet, praising murderers as saints. He had not had a dream of doves for a long time before this night. With sore fingers, he took the prayer book from the hiding in the wall and tried to make out the words in the candlelight.

The section on the offering started with the paragraphs on the incense service. He could never understand why the lamps were cleaned in the order of five and two; this order preceded burning of the incense. Incense offering was the holiest part of the service. It was a precious gift given to the Creator that was not paid for by taking life, causing pain to any living being. Shlomo wanted to be like incense and rise in a pillar of smoke into heaven and be praised for his passing through all four universes until the Throne itself. During the time while spices were burning on the altar, the suffering in seven firmaments was halted. This morning, at the dawn of his execution, Shlomo Molcho is praying that his suffering rectifies the damage caused by the exile; that his death counts towards the time of the ultimate redemption.

The Stranger on Ararat Street

Aviva was listening with her eyes wide open, the face flushing with wonder, anger, and fear. She was silent for a few minutes after Gabriel took a deep breath and reflected upon his long discourse. He was trying to explain his meetings with Yossi. The conversation was about all anxieties caused by the warning and speculations on other people involved.

Aviva is a well-grounded person. She would delve into work that encompasses studying esoteric texts and the lives of those who compiled them, but never lose grip on her astute perspective of existence. She went through some rough patches in her life and had battled betrayal, disappointment, and hostility. Regardless of the causes and effects of any tragic event, she never felt physically threatened by other people. Some people she interacted with were not the best kind, but never posed a danger to her wellbeing.

What she heard today made her think differently. The person Gabriel met in Tsfat and the Old City earlier was less of a threat and more of a tease. Regardless of the circumstances of those encounters, the entire episode was strange. There was an entirely surreal quality to it. She asked for Yossi's phone number and promised to inquire about him before making any conclusions.

Gabriel suggested going for a walk around the city before dinner. He wanted the sombre atmosphere after the conversation to dissipate. His wish was granted. In a few moments, they were light and carefree, strolled along Cardo towards the staircase to the Kotel.

They were invited for a meal by Aviva's friends and the troubling conversation was altogether forgotten. The dinner was enjoyable and with exquisitely prepared dishes

135

and wine. The party went on until late that night in a joyous atmosphere and singing. It was late, after midnight, when the group of guests from the dinner party set on a trip through poorly lit streets to their hotels scattered all over the Old City. As they were going up the stairs toward Ararat St., Gabriel turned around several times with the feeling that someone was following them. The neighbourhood was quiet and most residents asleep behind dark windows. At the last turn on Ararat St., he caught the glimpse of a person who walked at a short distance with head turned downward, staring at his feet while walking, obviously determined to avoid any eye contact. He walked too close to the party and almost hit Aviva with his elbow. Gabriel seemed alarmed by his presence and followed attentively every step the stranger made. He knew he would not be surprised if Yossi presented himself again. That the passer-by almost elbowed Aviva made him shiver from disgust and fear. They could not decide whether he looked like a native or a tourist, and even though there was enough time to memorise the details of his build, clothes, and hairstyle, it was almost impossible to determine his ethnicity, age, or reason for being in the street alone at that hour of the night. It was late when they reached the hotel near Yafo gate. The man disappeared in one arch off the Ararat St. He did not require their attention anymore. Not at that moment.

Yet Gabriel carefully jotted down all details of the evening related to the encounter on their way to the hotel. He would not hesitate about his look or the way he walked and the place he entered at the end of the walk on Ararat Street. And because of his newly gained habit to write pieces of information and file them in case they became necessary, he immediately recognised the man two days later. He saw him in the Shuk during the weekly grocery shopping. Aviva still emailed nothing about Yossi, and this new episode, though unnerving, did not have any meaning. He was waiting for the end of that week and her visit. Otherwise, Gabriel was getting ready for another meeting at the Beit-El scheduled at six in the morning on Friday.

'There is no one under this name registered at the number you used for Yossi. The account is under the name of the business in Tsfat. Yossi may or may not be the owner. That still means nothing. The phone may have been borrowed just for the occasion of your meeting. It would tell us nothing about the person who offered to guide you around the town. My friend is still trying to find out more about Yossi and his whereabouts. We will know next week. As for the second man, I would try to forget the episode on Shabbat and the Shuk. There are so many tourists in Jerusalem at this time of the year. Please do not let fear and anxiety take over. I remember him as he passed by and looked at us and almost hit me with his elbow but would read nothing into it. He might have been drunk. Yet another person walking from somewhere to a hotel. '–said the message emailed later in the week.

Gabriel was grateful for the easygoing and rational approach Aviva had to the situations that caused him to frown and sigh for hours after they took place. That is why he loved her. She would not be thrown out of balance and intimidated by Yossi and alike characters. He was angry with himself for being out of touch with the actual world out there.

Gabriel held Aviva in his arms for a long time before she fell asleep and then slid out of bed and placed a nicely wrapped gift box on the table so she should find it first thing when she wakes up later. It was early in the morning and he headed to Beit-El through quiet streets.

Myrrh

Myrrh was a core ingredient of the sacred anointing oil, not only the component of the incense formula. The oil was used to ordain the first priests serving in the Tabernacle, later in the Temple. It was used for anointing the kings.

Myrrh is the product of affliction. It is harvested by repeatedly cutting into the tree bark of the species known for their resin producing properties. Myrrh is the blood or the trees. Cuts that are made on these trees stimulate bleeding. Gum that runs from the incisions is waxy and coagulates quickly. After the harvest, it becomes hard and glossy. It is white or yellow and can be of clear or of misty consistency. Unfortunately, with all the knowledge of the process and trees that would render precious gum when bruised, the myrrh that was used in the anointing oil and incense formula dating from the journey through the desert was not the one known and used in modern times. Pliny the Elder writes about liquid myrrh, the ingredient of the holy incense, used in the Temple service. Liquid myrrh cannot be identified in today's herb and spice market.

Besides its use in an offering, or the essential part for the inauguration of leaders of the Jewish nation (both secular and spiritual) myrrh was a known analgetic used for toothaches and was added to oils and creams applied to ease pain from bruises and sores.

Traditional Chinese medicine describes myrrh as a plant-based ingredient that is bitter and spicy by taste. It is compounded in formulas for the issues with a heart, liver, and spleen because of its blood moving properties; it is believed that it even has the power to clear stagnant blood from the uterus.

Mrs. Molcho had the cabinet cut out of stone, limestone to be more accurate, made of the piece of rock brought by her father from Jerusalem. It was one of the few things that he considered precious. Mrs. Molcho told Uriel how her father worked with a chisel and a hammer until late at night for many weeks to cut the hole in the rock, smooth the edges and shape it into a box-like object that opened on the top so it could serve as a storage for something he got on his trip to the land. She or anyone else was not allowed anywhere near the rock. Only Rabbi Pesach would sometimes visit her father, and they stayed in the room with the box for a long time, studying and interpreting the scriptures. She asked her father only once in many years of helping with his business, and the response she got was the teary look in his aged and almost blind eyes and a raspy whisper:

'Something that cannot be found anywhere else in the world anymore. I have given it away. And it was taken back to where it belongs. Precious myrrh.'

She never asked again, as it obviously caused great pain to her father. He died a few months after this conversation. Out of respect, she has not come near and touched the stone box until her father was alive. When thirty days of mourning were completed, she started clearing some of his belonging but left the box on its spot and delayed even looking at it. Even the memory of the liquid myrrh that it contained made her open the lid with special care. That first time when she lifted the lid of the box, she got the whiff of the fragrance that was locked inside a cold, smooth surface. That too disappeared, and she never sensed it again.

Uriel heard this story but never wondered what could have been the secret that Mrs. Molcho's father took to the grave and never shared with his only daughter. If a spice merchant had something that was not supposed to be revealed to the undeserving souls, it was his duty to let it slip through his fingers. He was sure the time of revealing the secrets was at hand. Soon enough the scriptures related to the incense compounding would not have to be studied behind the locked door. There would not be any need to keep Ketoret hidden from the undeserving.

Uriel believed that even the minutiae of the Temple service made an impact in all seven firmaments. He did not question the disappearance of the liquid myrrh and could understand the passion of the spice merchant, and the life spent on learning about the incense; the reward of discovery of the most valuable ingredient and keeping it for a short time. He cared little about secrets and was more focused on incense used as a medicine. Uriel wanted to decode the remedial properties of substances and proportions in the formula. He was not keen on chasing after legends erased from the memory of the living.

The Proposal

During the third showing at the religious court at Beit- El, he understood the reason for being sent back and forth over the request for admission. The Rabbis finally provided the answers to the questions asked at the first meeting. Not that the Rabbis had any doubts about his life or family; they were reluctant to grant him the place at the academy for his lack of knowledge. He was behind in many areas of learning, making his progress doubtful. How would he fare in an environment with many setbacks? It is difficult to find a learning partner for an adult with little knowledge of the Torah. An accurate report will render that Gabriel does not understand Hebrew, cannot read Aramaic, never studied Talmud.

It would be difficult to find a learning partner for an adult student working on basic observances. Daily sessions were organised in pairs. Adult learners were paired according to the level of knowledge and learning preference. All students of his age were fluent in Hebrew and Aramaic. All students were well versed in scriptures, Jewish philosophy, and ethics.

Most of the students have already been married, and Gabriel has not even been engaged. This did not earn him trust and inspire much confidence of the community leaders reviewing the application. Rabbi Avichai said nothing. He asked a few questions and remained silent. The eyes of Rosh Yeshiva reminded Gabriel of his mother; nothing, he thought, decided, and said would be to his determent, Gabriel believed. The other two members of the court depended on Rabbi Avichai for any decisions and were looking for guidance in this matter. Following everything that was taken into consideration and mentioned above, Gabriel was granted partial admission–he would be tutored by one of the two Rabbis present at the meeting twice a week, make the best of effort to learn Hebrew and would look for the earliest opportunity to get married.

The last recommendation that was issued in the manner of a command brought a smile onto Gabriel's face. He hoped to meet someone special when he purchased the airfare to Tel-Aviv. Has it not been the hidden agenda from the beginning of his quest? He has been alone for the longest time. Occasional dating, short-lived relationships, brief disappointments, and retreat to his enchanted, lonely self filled him with resentment and sarcasm over the years. He has not enjoyed re-living past and feasting on memories of sentiments regardless of the meaning they brought to his life. He is here, in Beit-El, to break free from the vicious circle. He agreed and promised to work in the suggested direction at once.

Aviva woke up late that morning, surprised by the silence in the room. She was accustomed to the constant racket of her Tel-Aviv neighbourhood. Silence was only a brief mirage in her dreamy mind. When she got up to make a cup of coffee, the clamour of the street in full daylight, buzzing of insects at the window, doors opening and closing in the hotel corridor, and loud voices of the guests were all there and moved into the room after her senses stirred from sleep.

Most people start their day either with a cup of coffee or tea. Aviva was 'a-splash of-milk, one- sugar' type of person. Her calendar was packed on workdays. Friday morning was always filled with gratitude for precious moments when she could sip coffee and read the news without looking at her inbox or rush to leave home to drive to the office. She stretched and bent her neck left, right, back, and forth and then saw something wrapped in the gift paper on the kitchen countertop next to the coffeemaker. Should she open the box? She was both curious and hesitant about unwrapping it without Gabriel next to her. It must be that he wanted her to find the gift. Why leave it in the most prominent place in the room otherwise? She was certain that he wanted her to open it while she was alone before his return from the meeting. Maybe he was insecure and was afraid of her reaction or lacked confidence in the choice of a gift.

Without spending more time thinking about whether to wait, she pulled the bow, removed the paper, and opened the box. Tiny, golden cube covered with Hebrew letters all over glittered on the dark blue velvet cushion inside. She carefully lifted and turned it to look at all sides and tried to read the inscribed letters. It seemed to be a simple task; the letters were engraved as a long uninterrupted line around the cube. She tried to make out the words they spelled. They were etched in a way to tread a single line, curved on the edges, and wrapped around all sides with no space left uncovered. The longer she looked and pondered over the meaning, the more it eluded her. The letters moved before her eyes. They were wobbling and dancing; they flew off the box. Aviva put the golden box back on the table. She both admired and feared it.

Shortly after she had given up reading the letters on the golden cube, Gabriel pushed his head through the door. He saw her sitting with the unwrapped gift and a cup of coffee and quietly asked:

'Do you like it? I could not think of anything more beautiful to give you. Yes, I admit, the tiny treasure has a draining effect on the eyes.'- He said all that in one breath and eagerly waited for her response.

'I could not make out the words. What is the age and origin of craftsmanship? I could guess—late eighteenth or nineteenth century? Beautiful filigree work. Do you know what is inscribed on it?' - asked Aviva.

'Exodus 14, 19-21. They were used for the name of Seventy-Two. The name was known to the mystics since the most ancient times, discussed in the Zohar, Rashi's commentaries, but the use was written for the first time by Rabbi Abraham Abulafia, and there - you have it- in gold. It was crafted in Italy during the life of Ramchal (Moshe Chaim Luzzatto). I want to believe it was made by him.' - explained Gabriel.

'Where did you get it? It must be a precious family heirloom. Why did you give it to me?' - smiled Aviva.

She looked at him with fear and fire in her eyes. She was on the brink of tears and Gabriel rushed to put out the fire: 'There is no family, Aviva. I am the only one left of the family. I would not overestimate its value except for the weight in gold. It is valuable to me and a small circle of admirers of Jewish mysticism. I am not sure it should be displayed publicly because I do not know what it was used for. The scholars I have encountered did not know the purpose of that box. I thought you might be the best person to know about it, keep, and own it. In that way, you could become a family. My family. What do you think about this?'

Aviva was staring. Her mind came to a complete halt. It took a moment to think about what she heard. She blinked, but could not gather her thoughts. Just a few minutes before she tried to decode the inscription on the piece of gold. Also, Gabriel asked if she would marry him. The emotions were overwhelming, and she continued to stare at Gabriel in silence. Many years later she will tell her children about that morning, the three verses inscribed on the box; it did not feel real, and she was not fully aware of the words that slipped through her lips; she whispered:

'I would love to be your family.' Neither the question nor the answer passed for the proper way to propose. They were strange people solving mysteries. Gabriel and Aviva.

Next time when Gabriel sets his foot at Beit-El, he could share the fact that he was engaged. Therefore, the promise he gave to Rabbi Avichai was fulfilled. The couple spent the weekend in a state of complete peace with the world.

The Garden of Roses

My beloved has donned his festive clothes and will walk me down the rose path in the garden. The day has broken with the first rays of sunshine dancing on the soft flower petals. My beloved will meet me down on the rose path in the willow's shade; We will remember the time that filled us with a light of hope. I have been waiting for my beloved to walk me down the rose path in the garden. I have been waiting for a long time in the willow's shade. My beloved donned his festive clothes at the break of the day and left me waiting for him, alone and destitute, in the rose garden.

Vered, Zemora never stopped grieving the loss of her husband. Though she spent little time in his company and had to take care of their child on her own, she never internalised his death. The girl grew in the shadow of her dead father. Mother claimed she conversed with him every day, dreamt of him at night, and cried the rest of the time. Early in life, she had to summon her mother from the spells of despair–it was the most arduous task the child could imagine. She had to drag her mother back from the dreams of her brief happiness to the dread of reality. Her name gave the purpose of her entire life. Nehama (means comfort) lived to the expectations vested in her. As she was forced to fight for the attention of her misfortunate parent, Nehama perfected the ritual of bringing a smile to her mother's face.

Early in life, the girl learned to take care of herself, do the basic cooking, cleaning, and organise living space so their daily living could continue under the pretence of normality. When it was necessary, she made her mother search or buy food. When it was possible, they were given clothing items or fabric and they had to make the clothes themselves. Everything they had they owed to Rabbi Tzaitzak, who made sure they were safe and had sustenance. When the girl matured, a suitable suitor was found and Nehama got married. She moved to Salonica. Once left to her own devices, Vered Zemora wilted and died. No one called her back from the garden of roses, where she conversed with ghosts. There was no one to encourage her to eat and tell her to rest from crying. She faded away; turned into a translucent figure even before she passed into the realm where bodies did not matter. Rabbi Tzaitzak said she dissolved into the ocean of eternity. Vered Zemora was a special soul allotted a short time in this world with a sole purpose: to give birth to Nehama.

My beloved donned beautiful clothing to take me to the rose garden. We walked down the path together and rested in the shadow of the willows. It lasted few short moments, but I will keep the memory of light and hope forever.

Nehama gave birth to a son and named him Shlomo, after her father. When he grew up, he changed his family name from Avichai to Molcho to keep the memory of the martyr alive. His grandson was the one who spoke against Shabbatai Tzvi when hundreds of people followed him on the road to betrayal and madness. He could not find peace while surrounded by destroyers of truth. He warned the crowds of fervent followers of the false messiah:

'The redeemer will not give in to heresy.' The followers of Shabbatai did not heed to his warning. He was forced to leave the community and move away. Even though he was well of age, he picked up his possessions and moved with the entire family somewhere north of Salonica. No one has mentioned his name again, and the whereabouts of his sons and daughters are unknown. This is the brief history of three generations of direct descendants of

Shlomo Molcho. His legacy stayed with those who knew and understood the power of faith. While his memory still lived in the stories retold by a few, his children were kept hidden from the evil eyes of the world.

Those people who could understand the providence were navigated across the world from above. Physical distance and passage of time had little impact on them. Everyone will be summoned to the right place at the right moment in time.

In the next few weeks, Gabriel was occupied with the tedious business of settling down in the community of Beit-El; attended events, followed a different routine, got comfortable in his new home. He relied on help from new acquaintances and teachers. He spent weekends with Aviva. Surrounded by caring people who guided him every step of his way, he felt younger and did not feel isolated anymore. Life was good. Gabriel was at peace with the universe.

Costus

Saussurea Costus, commonly known as costus, kuth, or putchuk, is a species of thistle in the genus Saussurea. It is native to India and thrives in the Himalayan region. The plant can be grown in a wide variety of soils. In traditional Chinese medicine, its root is one of the fifty fundamental herbs used for treatment. In Ayurveda, it was used to help normalise and strengthen digestion, cleanse the body of toxic accumulations, enhance fertility, and reduce pain. Mystics of Kashmir ate this plant in abundance. The plant favours higher altitude for seed germination.

At the dawn of war, Uriel got a sizeable amount of costus harvested in the Himalayas. The merchant said it arrived with the last shipment before traffic halted. It was not possible to travel any more. He asked for an exorbitant amount of money and delivered the order in tar-lined boxes. The roots of the plants were like stone, hard and dry. This transaction took place in November 1940. The formula compounded from the shipment of costus would be the last one too. Uriel gently caressed the plants in Mrs. Molcho's apartment. The notes on items he bought, read, observed, and processed were laying on his desk at home. So far, he had filled 476 pages with instructions, drawings and journals kept on the visits to Mrs. Molcho. The extensive work included his thoughts and references to the scriptures that concerned the laws of Ketoret; his thoughts on what he learned from the scriptures and elsewhere. Sometimes, he included the prescription for teas, powders, and tinctures he had received from his elderly teacher. The notebook was the treasury of knowledge. It was as precious as gemstones. Hard work paid off, and his son's asthma attacks have subsided in intensity and frequency.

Alas, dangerous times were on the horizon. The pharmacist who had sent him to Mrs. Molcho made every attempt to move to Palestine. The last time they had run into each other, the elderly man looked exhausted and worried. He did not believe Greece, or any other Mediterranean country, had the military power on a par with the German army and expected fast advancement of the enemy and humiliating defeat of the Greeks and other countries fighting against the Germans in the region. Horrific stories about the fate of Jews in Germany and Poland could be heard in the community. They were stripped of civil rights, deported to labour camps, or enclosed in ghettos. The eyes of the elderly pharmacist filled with tears. Uriel wanted to offer words of comfort but could not find any and was silent and sad.

People with no roof above their head should not wait for the storm as an exercise in patience. Uriel knew that. He foresaw the tragic events that took place in the spring of 1941. Many people across Europe did. Very few could imagine, even as the worst nightmare, that one-third of the world Jewish population would perish in the storm of war. Jews and righteous Gentiles could not understand the indifference of the rest of the world to this calamity. Heaven had closed the gates of mercy and the angel of death was given the power over the destiny of millions. The old pharmacist rushed to Palestine in the autumn of 1940. He was one of the few to escape death in the camps.

Uriel and his family had left the town soon after they heard about ghettos in Poland and Ukraine. There were rumours that similar plans were drawn for the communities in Greece. It was difficult to move the family from one place to another. Adele was only a few months old. The money they had on them was disparaged. They used it until it lasted to purchase food. Shelter and silence of the families that accepted to hide them on their farms and houses were paid in gold.

There was little gold left; Uriel despaired. He had a hard decision to make. The paths they could take were few. The outcomes of taking each of them were easy to foresee. He tried to project any possibility that would save the entire family. There were none. Uriel tried to save the children, but no one wanted to risk being shot dead by the Germans. The time came when the family had to be broken. They left the youngest one with the family in Kozani. Adele was only eleven months old. She would remember none of them. The little one would not know who she is, her name or the names of her parents. She could not reveal them to the soldiers who would visit the farm.

Soon after they had left the city, Uriel understood the calamities that had befallen the community in Greece and anywhere else throughout Europe. It is human to respond to bad news with disbelief. He did not comfort himself and his family with false hopes. It was clear they were left with very few options. He did not think about the situation that was getting worse. Before strength abandoned him, all his energy was directed to planning and carrying out step after step in the everyday battle for survival. Uriel did not regret leaving behind his home and other possessions and reducing his daily activities to searching for food. His job was to find a safe way of travelling from one shelter to another. He learned where to find fresh eggs, who to purchase bread from, the skill of keeping the fire burning without excessive smoke. It was a lot of work with little result, and he knew their chances for survival crumbled with each day that passed in a constant movement from one place to another.

People use all their strength, skills, and brains when threatened with demise. They also rely on the community and family for help. Jews had none. They were left entirely to the mercy of heaven. And heaven was closed to their prayers.

The Photographs

Gabriel wanted to talk to Rabbi Avichai about the encounters with Yossi for a few weeks. He was looking for the right moment to divulge his impressions of the strange meetings with his strange acquaintance. Looking for the right moment proved to be a hard task. Finally, he was told the Rabbi was not overly busy and invited him in for a conversation. He wanted to know about his progress, his new life, his fiancé. They engaged in a long talk. Gabriel told him about Yossi while paying special attention to the warning issued during the last event in the Old City a few weeks before. What he had heard in response did not disperse his fears. It explained nothing. He was even more confused than before. Later he sent the message to Aviva, relaying the exact words exchanged in the conversation. This is what Rabbi Avichai said:

'Do you know the meaning of the Pardes? Four Rabbis took on the journey into the secret meaning of the Torah. Three of them failed to see and learn the truth, and the experience ended with their demise. Only Rabbi Akiva came out unscathed. Why? He had the most powerful faith of the four. He was humble. He did not gaze beyond his own limitations.'

'How does this reflect on the experience you shared with me? Even if I share my thoughts, and opinion, I may be wrong. When we do not have any clarity, we pray to get better at understanding. If we are fearful, we ask for the strengthening of faith. You should be patient. When clarity is delayed, patience can make up for it.'

Gabriel returned to his apartment late that night and found the entrance door open ajar. Instead of venturing into the new adventure on his own, he turned around and knocked on the door of the neighbour who lived in the apartment below him. He always returned greetings with a kind smile and offered to share food or a piece of news with Gabriel. The man was in his late seventies but looked much younger with his back straight, wide shoulders, cheerful eyes. He was babysitting his grandchildren three times a week and had quiet evenings on the other four days. Today was a quiet day, and Gabriel hoped he might still be awake and would not mind the doorbell at the late hour.

'Avi', Gabriel called while the door was still closed, 'someone broke into my apartment.'

Avi opened the door and rushed up the stairs with Gabriel. The drawers in the living room were dislodged, and the content was in disarray on the floor. There was not much to steal from the drawers. Gabriel had moved in six weeks before and was still working on furnishing the apartment in the new neighbourhood. They found that someone stole the photographs of his family. He had twenty black and white photos of Uriel, Rina, and the children - three of them were missing.

Avi returned to his apartment, and Gabriel was left alone with his thoughts and fears. He spent the rest of the night in the armchair, looking through the window into the bright, waning moon, and pushed the whole incident aside in his thoughts until morning.

There was no point in reporting the incident to the police. Three photographs were missing. He did not understand the interest a thief may have in the family photographs. Gabriel had lost nothing, as the copies of each item were kept in various archives and private files. He had taken all valuable parchments to the Beth-El earlier. The silver and the golden box were both at Aviva's.

The incident was too bizarre to share, though he talked about it with Aviva the next morning. She was silent and shaken more than Gabriel. He could feel her fear and disbelief over the phone; Aviva was reluctant to continue the conversation about the theft. She said she would like to talk longer when she arrives in town at the end of the week. That would be the day after their phone conversation. She also asked which photographs were taken, as they were all scanned earlier.

Gabriel returned to Rabbi's office in the afternoon but had not spoken about the event. Aviva told him that three photographs that were missing were taken a long time before his mother was born. They were the pictures of her sister as a baby, her brother not older than two. The occasion for the session was not clear; they were taken to preserve a milestone, a celebration. There was nothing about the occasion to be found among the other papers, and Adele was not aware of its importance. Her mother was beautiful in the pictures, with dark, luscious hair and dark eyes. Uriel was posing with a smile that turned his face into the epitome of happiness. The parents looked at each other in the second photograph, with a blue-eyed boy with fair hair between them and a baby seated comfortably on a silky cushion next to him. The little girl had a doll in her hands that was dressed in a lacy gown decorated with bids and pearls. The third photograph was of two children—they were both sitting on the chesterfield with hands placed on their hips; they did not look thrilled; The baby could burst into tears at any moment and the boy was caught between frowning and giggling and had not opted for any of the two when the photographer snapped the picture.

Aviva and Gabriel were pondering over the reasons for the break-in and theft. They did not come up with any plausible answer until the end of the weekend. The mystery reached the climax when Gabriel found an envelope tucked under the door on Tuesday evening of the following week. The photographs that were taken a few days earlier were packed into the brown envelope and pushed under the door. The person interested in his family history obviously had a complete disregard for the encounter with the police. Possible public humiliation or physical harm would not scare him. The matters of reason and basic decency could not stop him from breaking into the apartment and stealing, so he could enjoy the photographs for a few days.

This made Gabriel cringe in his bed at night and look over the shoulder whenever he walked outside. He would turn around a few times before entering his building or other places. Yet he did not speak about this with anyone else, nor did he consult people who helped him in the past. Gabriel respected the advice of his teacher this time: he waited for the unfolding of the circumstances that would help solve this and other mysteries that had tormented him over the years.

It was Aviva who did not cease to investigate the strange events cropped up since Gabriel had set his foot in Tsfat. However, she kept her lips tight on the matter. She did not want to say anything that could cause more anxiety and frustration to both of them.

At first, she thought the meetings with Yossi were arranged by one of the civil or military security agencies. They were routinely done when someone with Gabriel's family history and background spent a few months in Israel. Unfortunately, that was not the case. The query on Yossi ended with one and only learning centre in Tsfat. She wondered about the name and the number Gabriel had; the phone was not registered in that name, as previously concluded. She connected to someone who could help with information on the community and discovered that a small learning group did not share in the regular schedule of communal activities. They were separated, gathered around their Rabbi and acted secretively about their meetings. Her source promised to help her identify 'Yossi' by the description Gabriel provided. He has not returned with any results for a few weeks.

Aviva was not a religious person according to the established standards of the religious communities in Israel. Those communities are leery of the secular people; some even oppose everyday communication with secular Israelis. This is even more obvious when secular people want to discuss issues related to religious observance. Aviva could not find out anything related to Yossi on her own. She had to contact someone who had better knowledge of plausible reasons for his interest in Gabriel Marcus.

The plan required more time and involvement. If she wanted questions answered, she had to ask the right people. She contemplated who to ask for help. Those who could were people who will demand something in return. They may ask her to share every detail about the relationship with Gabriel, and Aviva did not want this. She thought of travelling to Tsfat on her own and try to find Yossi and press him for answers. Of course, she knew this would be the least productive move and could end in an embarrassing situation for everyone involved. Then she remembered her old friend from town.

Safta Yocheved

Safta Yocheved was a figure that many Tsfat residents still mention in their conversations, though she passed away in the 1970s. She was born to a religious family that strongly believed in coming of the Messiah, the anointed one, the Redeemer. The woman must have been familiar with parts of Zohar that claim that Messiah would start his journey in Meron and visit some other places on the road to Jerusalem. The exact place in Meron is the tomb of the Lamp (Rabbi Shimon Bar Yohai). The route goes through Tsfat and ends in a grand finale by passing through the east gate (the one filled with stones by the Ottomans) onto the Temple Mount. She was concerned with the strenuous physical effort of this trip. Of course, the Messiah, regardless of his holiness, would get thirsty. Therefore, Safta Yocheved prepared a plate with cookies and pastries and a cup of tea in expectation of his arrival. Every day she would sit in front of the house with the tea and cookies, waiting for the beloved traveller to show up on a road from Mt. Meron. When she died, the place where she was sitting with the treats was named the Lane of the Messiah.

The great-grandson of Safta Yocheved was Aviva's friend from childhood. He was a joyful and gentle hoodlum who pulled her hair in school and named her names that caused much laughter among classmates and tears to Aviva. He still lived in town and operated the construction business. They met in Tel-Aviv a few months before. Despite his teasing, he was a good-hearted person. Aviva remembered Izzy invited her out for a meal when she found time in Tel-Aviv or anywhere else. Aviva was waiting for her friend in a small restaurant close to the museum one evening in Elul. He arrived a few minutes late. The traffic slowed him down.

Aviva was reluctant to show excitement over the meeting. She tried to talk about the case of Yossi but had to insert it into the context of her and Gabriel's relationship. She did not mention the photographs and the break-in incident. Izzy listened intently. As she was speaking, his face turned into a frown. He continuously nodded and bit his lip, but kept quiet. When she exhausted all the words on the matter, he said:

'Aviva,' he said, in a deep, hushed voice, 'I know the place you mentioned, and I, too, heard about the group of people that may be interested in Gabriel. They are harmless. I will try to get in touch with someone who could shed light on a reason anyone would have for following him around. I may not do this right away.'

He called her a week later and spoke with excitement. The news was about the friend of a friend who helped him get in touch with the head of the community that Yossi might have been involved with. He wanted to share the information but not on the phone, and he would not mind meeting in Jerusalem with her and Gabriel and deliver the results of the inquiry.

Izzy, Aviva, and Gabriel were sipping tea and eating biscuits just a few days after the conversation about Izzy's meetings in Tsfat. He delivered the results of his investigation. What he said made little sense to Gabriel. The Rabbi said that there was a small group of men who learned long hours every day and had different routine than the others in the community for the reasons he did not want to discuss. One of these men from the group might have met Gabriel in Tsfat. He was not sure about the fake name. There was a man named Yoslimon, and he might have used the short version of his name.

Izzy shared his impression that this community knew, expected, and waited for Gabriel to arrive in Tsfat. This was strange. Only Aviva knew some details of his trip to Tsfat.

The Game of Chess

Life resembles the game of chess. We have to follow the
rules. We need a strategy to end the game victorious. The
victory depends on the strength of the opponent, as well
the knowledge and perseverance that have to be employed
to fight and win. Besides, the game has to be played with
respect and in silence.

Aviva realised that business with Yossi slowly turned
into the chess game. All moves she made sent her in one
direction: the secluded group of mystics in Tsfat. Shake
them down. That was the only move she could think
of. With that goal in mind, she embarked on a scouting
expedition to the town. Summer was followed by the
holiday season. The right time for the visit would be two
to three weeks after the last festival.

On a beautiful day in late October, Aviva drove to
Galilee with one destination on her mind: a two-storey
building on the outskirts of the town. It was a modern
edifice, all built of concrete and glass. The facade did not
have lines of any known style, and little to attract the
attention of the visitors. She parked and stared at the
building, contemplating the excuse to be let in.

An elderly woman was walking across the parking lot
to the entrance. She was dressed in the manner of women
in the Chasidic community, with a skirt covering most
of her shins, comfortable, layered top and tightly fitting
scarf on her head. Aviva called out from the car, inquiring
about the Rabbi she wanted to meet. The woman stopped,
glanced at her, then continued to walk to the building
without providing an answer.

This would be a sufficient reason for most people to get
upset with the person, the place, or even themselves. Aviva
was used to exclusive, odd, and sometimes even offensive

attitude of the most religious members of Israeli society. She found someone who would not be visibly different from the people congregating around the synagogue. Izzy agreed to meet with her for lunch later in the day, and she asked for the time of the meeting to be pushed, so they could find the Rabbi. He arrived at the parking lot shortly after the call and greeted her with a broad smile. A few minutes later, Izzy waved to her from the door and called for her to join him.

Aviva expected to meet an elderly man with a long beard, Borsellino hat, and grey suit. That would be the traditional attire of this Chasidic group. When she opened the door, she saw a young man who politely nodded in her direction but did not look at her. He did not have a long beard. Aviva was wearing white linen pants, and he would not look at her. He was listening intently to her discourse. Aviva continued to talk for the next twenty minutes with eyes welded on the Rabbi, analysing his eyes, face, hands. Anything that would render the intention to hide that he understands and knows what she was talking about. He listened, but did not show that any part of her monologue aroused any emotions. At the end of Aviva's long report on the events, he stayed quiet for a few moments. Then, he said in response:

'I did not want to interrupt while you were speaking; however, I am familiar with the person mentioned as well as the situation that troubles you and your fiancé. Yossi (Mr. Rothstein) has been acting according to my instructions.'

Aviva gasped loudly, not being able to control her surprise. 'But how? Why?'

'I would not like to cause more anxiety to you and your fiancé, but will give you the number that you can call and find the help if needed. Judging by the information provided today, you may need help.'

'What kind of help?' whispered Aviva.

'You will understand when it is needed. Yossi meant well. So do I.'

They quietly found the way out of the room and into the building and went to their cars in silence. There was a lot to discuss during a meal following the meeting with the Rabbi.

Aviva suddenly did not feel like talking. She felt completely exhausted and confused. She was under an adrenaline rush for about an hour and just wanted to lie down and curl up. She asked Izzy to wait for her at home and headed to a place from her childhood–the memorial park of Gam Zu Ish.

The tomb and the surrounding grounds were always enveloped in greenery. Perennials kept the shade and filled the air with a refreshing scent of its resin. Aviva almost fell asleep, lulled by the crickets and gentle breeze in the canopies of the trees above. She was reminiscing on other visits to this place throughout the years of her life in Tsfat, when she came to play, or rest, or simply to be on her own and dive deep into thoughts like today.

'Aviva!' the voice that called her name was familiar and for a moment she thought she was dreaming. 'Aviva, wake up!' the voice urged her to open her eyes and thus she knew she was not dreaming.

She got out of the sweet slumber that lasted a few minutes and looked in the person's direction. Then, she jumped in surprise; her ex-husband, Ilan, was standing in front of her. She saw him last time many years ago when he met with her to complete the divorce process. They have not been in touch since, and she did not even know where he lived and what his job had been. She had not expected to meet him in Tsfat, of all places on that day.

'Ilan? What are you doing here?' she did not hide her emotions. She was trembling inside, and her fingers were cold and shaky. This was not the moment to exchange the pleasantries. Over time, she lost any interest in his whereabouts. He worked for the army. That is all she knew.

'Aviva, I just wanted to tell you. Warn Gabriel, your fiancé, to keep his eyes wide open. Less he shares about him (what he learns, where he goes, or people you socialise with) the better. Even the information about his plans for the weekend with you, or places you visit together, should be kept between two of you.'

'But why? Why are you telling me this? What is going on?' Aviva's eyes were wide open, and she was gasping for air. There was a storm raging inside her, and many conflicting emotions and thoughts were searching the way to be turned into questions.

'There is not much going on right now, and you and Gabriel should do your best to keep it that way, as I am not sure if I can watch over him all the time.' Ilan handed her the phone number written on the back of the business card.

'Call this number only if you notice you are followed. Do not call me on your or Gabriel's phone.'

'I cannot leave this place and end the conversation on this note. You show up after five years of complete silence and warn me about the safety of my fiancé, yet do not want to disclose why we would have to worry about it. What is going on?'

'If I told you now, you may not have more clarity than me, and I would have to go into sharing some information that I am not supposed to share. I am asking you to trust me and follow my advice. That is all. I wish you and Gabriel well.'

He turned and left after he literally pushed the paper with the number into her hand. Aviva watched him walk past the shrubbery and the trees until he disappeared. She felt weak and feverish. Instead of a meal, she asked Izzy's wife for a cup of tea and passed out on the couch in their living room.

Gabriel tried to call Aviva several times but could not get through. When she called back, it was late in the evening and her voice sounded distant and tired. She said she was not feeling well and took the day off but will drive to Jerusalem in the morning and rest there. She still did not mention the visit to Tsfat, conversation with Izzy, meeting with the Rabbi, and most of all, the encounter with Ilan.

Frankincense

Mrs. Molcho locked the door of her apartment and hung the note for anyone that may look for her: 'Please do not knock. All orders are to be handed in person to Mr. Tzelidis, the caretaker.'

There would not be any more orders, she knew that. Most of the people from the neighbourhood and elsewhere were gone. She turned and looked one more time at the building and got into the car that took her to the mountains in the north. She had a small suitcase with her clothes and a bag full of frankincense that would pay for her safety.

It is another precious gift of the trees taken by inflicting pain. The tears of the trees. Pure and genuine. The only valuable possession that she carried along. The prescriptions and lists of plants were at Uriel's place. He promised to hide them or give them to someone who would take them to Israel if he failed at safekeeping. Mrs. Molcho was holding the bag of frankincense with her fingers pressing firmly against the fabric.

Many centuries ago, the father of Vered Zemora was trying to keep the bag full of frankincense safe while travelling the land and sea in the hope to reach Tsfat and start a new life there. The sac of precious resin enabled him and his only child to find a home, pay for the food and anything else needed.

The roads and landscapes differed from the one Mrs. Molcho was passing by, but the motifs were the same; the owners of the frankincense had to leave everything behind and set on a journey to survive.

Uriel handed his notes, prescriptions and lists to the pharmacist who left Salonika on the last ship that sailed from the port to Cyprus and further to Palestine. At the time he was the only one entrusted with the legacy of spice compounders dating back to the community in Spain and possibly earlier. The practices and formulas Mrs. Molcho inherited from her father could be attributed even to Rambam; over seven hundred years before she packed the frankincense into the linen bag, wrapped it in wax paper, placed it in a sac for easy carrying. It had to be handled with care. Exposure to different temperature and moisture could have been harmful. It was supposed to be kept in a dark, dry, cool, but not cold place. Jars made of thick glass or glass boxes lined with limestone. The constant temperature was important and should not be changed even during the hot days of summer, which was achieved by storing the most sensitive ingredients for her prescriptions into boxes made of limestone, marble, and granite. The precious substance could be violated by air, travels on the country roads, and even anxious thoughts that could not have been helped and turned away.

The man who promised to keep Uriel's notes and prescriptions safe did not have the time to look at the content of the package tied loosely with a ribbon and tucked in the suitcase that was taken to storage with other meagre possessions saved from the pillage of German soldiers.

When he finally went through everything, he found journals, notes, and hundreds of lists of plants with names in Hebrew and Latin. It took him a few days to put everything in order; He immediately directed his quest back to Greece. Uriel handed him the fruit of diligent work performed over many years. Without delay, former owner of the pharmacy on Hagia Sofia set on a search for Uriel and his family. Even though he did not know the exact place of their hiding, he was certain that the family had not left Greece at that point. They must have been wandering from place to place in constant search for safety and shelter. Through his contacts, he found they were hidden on the farm near Kozani for a few weeks. He asked his friends to hand Uriel the letter with a brief message:

'I found someone who will take your boy. Do not share with anyone. Send your son with the carrier of this message at once.'

Adela's brother was smuggled into the cargo ship and travelled for weeks through the Mediterranean until he reached the port of Jaffa. By the time he landed at his destination, his parents and sister were deported to the death camp. He was ten years old when he boarded the ship in Salonika on a warm October night. During the few weeks of the journey across the seas, he grew old. When he arrived in Tel-Aviv, he did not want to remember his childhood anymore.

PART FIVE

The Hackers

Aviva told Gabriel everything about her secret visit to Tsfat the day before. She described to the minutia her conversation with Ilan. She told him who Yossi is and his interest in Gabriel's adventures in Israel. As she was speaking, Gabriel's face was growing more solemn. He tried to weigh up each word before making conclusions. He had changed his perspective of the events following the conversation with the Rosh Yeshiva.

'I understand I am being followed around. I am denied any insight into the understanding of the clandestine affairs that involve me. A few people dropped a line of what seemed to be the explanation but never fully disclosed facts that would help me resolve this most disturbing situation.'–Gabriel tried to sound calm. However, his chin was shaking and his eyes filled with tears.

Aviva understood past events were taxing on his nerves but could not offer comfort. Not after the meeting with Ilan. Gabriel continued:

'I learned there were at least two individuals or groups that monitor any step I take, any movement I make at all times. This is an intimidating and unnerving situation I have to live with every day. I hope you realise that regardless of repeated attempts to resolve this quandary, it got only more confusing and exasperating.'

'How does Ilan know what I was up to? What does he do, anyway? How long has he been involved? Why should I trust him?'–He has thrown the questions in her direction without offering the chance for answers.

'He works for the army.' Aviva said calmly, 'Israeli army. He is not just an ordinary soldier, but an officer with the rank. He can be trusted. The fact he had shared little only underlines his intention to help yet does not compromise his position as an intelligence officer.'- Aviva felt insulted by suspicions concerning Ilan's integrity.

'What about Yossi? His appearance is even more of a mystery and difficult to unravel. He mentioned something about the anticipation of my arrival. No one except you knew about my plans to visit Tsfat.' said Gabriel in a more agreeable tone.

'You underestimate the ability of hackers to get into your computer and explore the content of your emails. There is no mystery involved in the ways they gained the access to information; you should be concerned over their interest in you. Ilan did not want to expound on the matter. He was brief and clear but said nothing except what was necessary to deliver the message.'

'You mean—warning about the threat to my well-being. It made me feel even worse about the encounters with strangers anywhere I go.'

'No one said that you should fear for your life. Be watchful. Cautious. Mindful. You do not have to stay indoors and cover the windows with thick drapes. We will try to find the reason Yossi was following you around, the stranger in the Shuk, the stolen photographs. Mind you, anything that surfaces as the truth behind unusual events could be trivial and far from the dangerous or menacing plot of your enemies. I have the feeling there is nothing to worry about.'

She said that only to end the painful conversation. Aviva was not disturbed less than Gabriel.

Kibbutznik

Benjamin had to mature fast. His soul has turned old on the ships. His body followed a few years later. At first, his arms grew long, fingers fine and tender. Then he hit the height that surpassed anyone around by the time he turned fifteen. Being on a diet of mostly lentils and nuts, this was a surprise. His complexion grew dark from the constant exposure to the sun, but his silhouette was ghostly. Around that time, he fell in love with swimming; took on a daily practice of a few hours, and long limbs were soon bridled with muscles. His athletic body earned him more respect among peers, yet he made few friends. Benjamin was a secluded, secretive, and stern character. His blue coloured eyes that were beaming from the suntanned face complimented taciturn character and sadness that kept his heart locked for everyone.

The pharmacist had not disclosed his reasons for saving Benjamin to anyone until the deathbed. He could have attempted to do the same for any other child. Was it the gratitude for Uriel's trust that compelled him to act? The death pit swallowed his entire family shortly after the boy was smuggled as a stowaway on board a cargo ship in Salonica. He paid little attention to the destiny of the family after the war, assuming the boy was a complete orphan. In the years that followed the announcement of the statehood of Israel, Benjamin had joined one of the Zionist kibbutzim and was brought up in the secular environment.

The community was tending the vineyards and grew other food for their daily needs. Benjamin learned how to make spiced wine. He became the sole proprietor of the recipe for mulled wine with cinnamon and citrus fruit that was ordered for Passover from Bet-El community in Jerusalem. He married in his early thirties and had a daughter and a son. The years of his childhood spent in Salonica were hovering over him like a dream.

Then he discovered he was not the only family member that survived the Holocaust. The shadows of the times past he wanted to keep locked in the darkest room of his memory were tormenting him with regret, self-pity, and sorrow. He learned that his sister, the baby he vaguely remembered, was not taken to the camp, neither murdered with others, but lived safely close to Salonica. Distant relatives of their mother adopted her after the war. They have picked Adele up from the family in Northern Greece who hid her for four years. He did not learn more and did nothing to find her. He never shared this with his wife and children.

One day his daughter told him she heard the Diaspora museum offered access to the public to data stored in their archives. They had the largest file on the history of Sephardi communities, from the first expulsions to mass prosecutions in Spain and Portugal. She visited the archives and found the research funnelled by Prof. Vasiliadis and Gabriel to Tel-Aviv museum. She thought she found someone that could be related to their family. Benjamin, who was over seventy years old, listened to the story about miracles retold by his daughter. Tears ran down his face, and he kept murmuring: 'It is too much, too much...'

He did not interrupt her. He said nothing, just sat petrified, lost in his thoughts. Then he sprang to his feet, lift the fist towards the sky and said: 'I do not need that now. It is too late.'

He spent the last days of his life sipping on the wine laced with cinnamon and did not ask questions about Adele and Gabriel.

Hadassah, his daughter, let her father end life as he wished—ignoring the ghosts of his childhood that suddenly sprang to life and ruined the tranquil routine of his days. Once he was gone, Hadassah tried to find out more about their family history. She started the quest in the Diaspora museum. She got some leads for the community in Serbia. It was too late. Adele Marcus died shortly after Benjamin. The address Hadassah got through her channels was wrong, and her letters returned unopened. This did not prevent her to continue the search. There was a story she learned about her late Aunt Adele; the trail of death and misfortune that followed her throughout life, except for time with the family in Greece. Ella and Shmu (Estelle and Samuel Lebel) were preparing to move to Israel just as Adele started her university studies but tragically died in a car accident. She had a loving marriage with her husband; he died of a stroke just as Gabriel turned eighteen. Hadassah was thinking about these calamities, grateful for her life that was simple and peaceful. The trajectory of her journey was running along sandy beaches of the Mediterranean Sea, under the bright skies of Israel.

She never gave up searching for Gabriel. Before he arrived in Tel-Aviv, she even asked for help from her brother. It turned out to be a cause for discord, altercation, and silence between siblings.

Enfant terrible

A few words about the son of Benjamin, son of Uriel. Hadassah, the older child, was loyal, agreeable, and diligent character since early childhood. Efraim–the opposite of his sister. The 'enfant terrible' nicknamed by one of his elementary school teachers, did not enjoy school, was always ready to play pranks on any classmate or neighbour, seldom engaged in anything other than games of soccer every day of the week. He grew healthy and happy, oblivious to the occasional shame and pain he caused to his family. Long years of learning and pursuing achievements in academia did not attract him. After serving the army, he got lucky in business deals with newcomers from Russia and local Arabs and soon amassed a small fortune. Thus, he failed the expectations of the acquaintances and neighbours. They thought he would keep low paying blue-collar job, if any.

Efraim beat all the naysayers. He lived in a three-bedroom apartment on Rothschild Boulevard and owned another one in Herzliya. No one knew what exactly his business was and when Hadassah confronted him and would not give up on the answer, he came up with the story about trading wine from Cyprus, some mineral cosmetic from Dead Sea salts and Carshina soap from Yemen. She had the impression that this story or the merchandise he traded was only a small part of her brother's business dealings. The other made him a perfect henchman for tracing Gabriel's steps throughout the Land. The stranger that walked behind the party of Shabbat guests or the one who 'borrowed' the photographs from Gabriel's apartment in Jerusalem were the people he was working with. They worked for him to be more accurate.

Hadassah did not know that Gabriel got engaged and lived in Jerusalem. Her brother did not tell her about the photographs or that he had him followed. Yet she finally found him. Years of perseverance paid off.

Once she learned the whereabouts of Gabriel in Jerusalem and his connections to the community of Beit-El on Rashi Street, Hadassah decided on a surprise visit. She contemplated approaching him in the street at first. However, that venue had many downsides; he might be frightened; strangers around them may overhear the conversation; he may not take it seriously. She knew nothing about Efraim's clandestine undertakings with breaking into the apartment of his cousin and hiring stooges to follow him around on other occasions. She also did not know that someone else had a keen interest in Efraim, his business, and his whereabouts. The spy was spied upon. Ilan knew about the photographs even before discussing the incident with Aviva in Tsfat. All these people were nervous about the encounters with strangers, coincidences that were well-planned projects, and all kinds of causes that inspired interference in the lives of others. They were uninvited and unwanted.

Reunion

Hadassah did not have any ill feelings for her family history. She was unaware of the recent turmoil and Aviva's trials at the investigation of Yossi. She bravely knocked on Gabriel's door one Sunday morning. Gabriel was awake for a few hours; He just returned from the morning prayers. The knock on the door was loud and resolute and broke the mellow silence of the room. He did not recognize the woman standing at the apartment door and cautiously asked how he could help. She insisted on talking to him. Gabriel did not want to open the door and excused himself, asking for a phone number to contact her later.

He called two hours after the surprise visit. Hadassah went into a long monologue about her father, the family, and everything that she did to find Gabriel. He seemed unimpressed. After a moment of silence, he promised to call her back and hang up. He called Aviva at once and shared the news of the day. He wanted her to be present at the next meeting with Hadassah.

Later that week, Hadassah, Gabriel, and Aviva were sitting in the living room at Gabriel's place and talked about their parents, Adele and Benjamin, children of Uriel. They tried to evoke the memories but realized that they did not have any. There was little in the lives of the cousins that connected them. Gabriel was wary of sharing the intimate memories of his mother; Hadassah was ashamed of the attitude her father took when he was informed of the whereabouts of his sister. Instead, they re-told the stories picked from Diaspora museum files. The conversation was forced and lacked warmth.

Aviva was useful in giving directions. She provided the dates related to the stories and names of those who made into them. She knew everything about the ships used to smuggle Jewish refugees into the Land; she knew about the kibbutz that was Benjamin's home for most of his youth; the schools Hadassah and Efraim attended, winemaking for Passover. She was the most enthusiastic person of the three sitting in Gabriel's apartment; the one that did not have to struggle with the feeling of awkwardness, regret, and embarrassment.

That was not the end to the reunions that evening. After an hour into their rendezvous, there was a loud knock at the door. Gabriel rushed to open before pounding disturbed the neighbours. He looked through the crack in the door and faced Efraim. The visitor greeted him with a broad, charming grin, grabbed his hand and shook it before it was extended. He walked into the apartment without being invited. Gabriel was watching as Efraim made his way into the living room and wondered at his brazenness and ease. He was relaxed and moved around Gabriel's place as his own. That may not be the first time his cousin visited, Gabriel thought.

The rest of the evening was spent reminiscing about Hadassah and Efraim's childhood on the kibbutz. The party went late into the night, and when the visitors left, Gabriel kept silent for a long time. Hadassah was livid with her brother. She did not share the idea of connecting to Gabriel and Aviva. She did not inform him about the visit, the address of Gabriel's apartment. She asked through her teeth clenched in anger: 'How did you know I would visit today?'

He did not answer. Efraim waved at her with a smile and disappeared into the side street. He had to rush to another venue before heading back home to Tel-Aviv.

'Call me tomorrow evening,' he echoed from the shadows of the alley. 'We will talk about everything.'

Hadassah was familiar with his habit of asking for a call or a meeting that never occurred. He would tell her to call and would not answer. That was his way of wiggling out of her company. He always did this in the most obvious and disrespectful manner.

Aviva shrugged her shoulders at Gabriel's suggestion that Efraim was the one who broke into the apartment a few weeks before. It did not matter. She was not interested in the episode with photographs. She was curious about Ilan's investigation and anything he had on Efraim. People do not get in the focus of Shin Bet for trading cosmetics and amber from Jordan. There was not a simple way to find the answers to those questions. Until she did, Efraim was to be kept at a distance.

'I am not comfortable around Efraim. I did not enjoy his company,'- said Aviva. They ended the conversation and decided not to schedule any meetings with Hadassah or her brother. Not until they get the answers to the questions that bothered them.

Nightmares

Anna turned her vivid dreams into poetry. She did not tell anyone about the contraption that churned out monsters in her nightmares. The images of unnamed demons had not left her alone until she started writing about them. That was the only way she could go through sleepless nights. The darkness from within poured outside and made her shiver from the uneasy feeling that something from the other side crossed into 'here' and 'now' of her existence. Once she had nightmares locked into words on paper, she would simply burn them and would feel temporary relief from pain and fear. She never shared this with anyone. Words on the paper that turned into ashes did not prevent nightmares from coming back. The routine only strengthened her ability to cope. She had the feeling of control over fear, the grip on the invisible tormentors—at least for a limited time. When she was composed and calm, she could approach them with a keen mind and understand the messages carried from dreams to reality. She discerned three recurring entities that frequented her nightmares; all three would be announced by a roar. Their names would be sounded each time they appeared. She remembered the names well. After being pronounced, the owner of the name would appear. The apparitions had eyes bright as fiery coals, did not use speech, but screamed out whatever they had to say and could cross great distances at the wink of an eye. Time did not stop them from moving back and forth through centuries and millenniums. The celestial forces in her nightmares kept asking the same question repeatedly; the question she could not answer: Do you know the number of the letters in my name? The answers she delivered were received with dismay and threats. She did not know the answer that will free her from the shadows of darkness that paid her visits every night since she met Gabriel.

Ever since they spent the night together in his family cottage, alone and very much in love, the nightmares moved into her life. The summer night in the forest was magical. The perfect season for love. Yet, their closeness set something into motion, released the powers that Anna P. could not control. She was thinking of sharing her terrible nightmares with Gabriel, but the right moment for this never came. Their love has always had limitations. It was a love of curiosity, the attraction of the young age, the intellectual challenge at moments; many words remained buried in both of them. The muted and mutual understanding of the boundaries. Lack of trust? That was not the lack of trust. They collided with the lines that were set in stone long before Gabriel and Anna were allotted their time, the measure of the words and names they carried.

Anna P. wrote about the music of her soul and left it for Gabriel to read-only when she crossed into a different universe. Then he may understand. He would finally see who she is. The veil with a golden thread and a velvet gown in hues of sage colour will make her beautiful and desirable in his eyes. He will know her real name. He will whisper that name to her, and she will use it to silence the angels that have been torturing her for centuries. Their questions will be answered, and they will be released and returned to the world of creation. She will finally be at peace.

Maaleh Ashan

There was a lot that he wanted to share with the world, no matter how imperfect and indifferent people around him may have been. The guards have placed a rope around his neck and pulled it whenever he lifted his head, so he kept it low. The king sent him a message: He could spit into the mirror and return to the herd of swine. He would be granted life. That was the last message from the throne. He was burnt alive on the frosty December morning. The messenger returned with the spit on his face. He was approached by the priest and asked if he wanted to confess and repent.

'I have already repented.' He bluntly denounced the offer. 'For my parents, too. I will not use my soul as a currency.'

'I have already repented.' His steps were getting heavier and slower. They had to prop him and carry him to the stake.

'Aaron shall burn upon it the incense spices every morning; when he cleans the lamps, he is to burn it. And when Aaron ignites the lamps in the afternoon, he is about to burn it.'

'The cleaning of the five lamps precedes the dashing of the blood of the continual offering; the blood of the continual offering precedes the cleaning of the other two lamps, the cleaning of the two lamps precedes the incense...'

In the veil of flames and smoke that formed around his body, he saw a shimmer of light entering the Temple. The light approached five lamps that were cleaned and lit by blowing lightly into their wicks. Then it moved to blood from the offering sprinkled in two corners of the sanctuary. It hovered over blood as the harvester examining the sheaves. It was good and of pleasant fragrance. The shimmer of light spread across and over the room, and the remaining two lamps were lit. He heard the voice: It is good. It is all for good.

Shlomo Molcho was rejoicing in the terrible moment of his death. He did not feel pain anymore. He pronounced the seventy-two letters of the Name. At once, his body turned into the pillar of smoke and dispersed into the air.

The House of Avtinas

According to the scriptures, the House of Avtinas, the priestly family responsible for compounding the incense, kept the identity of Maaleh Ashan a secret which became lost following the destruction of the Second Temple in 69 or 70 CE. Maaleh Ashan was the last of the fifteen ingredients listed for the incense formula. In tractate Sheqalim Rabbi Akiva tells a story about Shimon Ben Loga, who saw a child from the house of Avtinas. Shimon Ben Loga was harvesting the herbs when he met the child from the House of Avtinas. He saw the child cried and then laughed. He asked him:

'My son, why did you cry?'

'Because of the glory of my Father's house that has decreased.'- He responded.

'And why did you laugh?'

'Because of the glory prepared for the righteous in the future.'- The child said.

I asked, 'And what did you see?'

'The herb Maaleh Ashan is growing next to me.'

There is a well-known story that clarifies the dialogue above:

The House of Avtinas was to compound the Ketoret for the Holy Temple. They refused to teach anyone else trade secrets involved in producing the formula. The community leaders were worried about the formula being lost over time and requested the list of exact ingredients from the House of Avtinas. They refused to comply with the request. Time passed, and the issue was not resolved. The community leaders tried to undercut the House of Avtinas. They brought in specialists from Egypt who were experts in mixing spices and herbs. They wanted to punish the House of Avtinas for refusing to comply with the order of the religious court to share their formula for the Ketoret. The Alexandrian experts could make a mixture that duplicated the aroma of the Ketoret, however, they did not know how to make the smoke of the burning incense rise in a straight column which is accomplished by adding a small amount of Maaleh Ashan to the mixture. The smoke from the incense mixed by the experts from Alexandria dispersed all over the room rather than rise in a straight column.

The Torah scholars went back to the House of Avtinas and again demanded that they reveal the secret ingredient that made the smoke go up straight. Again, they refused and kept the secret to themselves. The community leaders had no choice but to rehire the family of Avtinas to be in charge of the Ketoret manufacture. Talmud relates they sent them a message to tell them they had their job back, but they refused to come. The community had to double their salary before they would take their job back. When they finally came back, the Torah scholars asked them:

'Why did you refuse to teach others how to do this?'

They answered: 'We have a tradition that the Temple will be destroyed. We are afraid that this information will fall into the hands of inappropriate people who will make Ketoret to serve idols. That is why we keep the secret in our family.'

Nobody believed. Yet, the Temple was destroyed.

Clarity

'Nu, how is your learning?' asked Rosh Yeshiva.

Gabriel respectfully stood up from his seat and greeted him.

'It could be better, thank you. I have to help my wife with the baby and housework and do not spend as much time learning as I should,' said Gabriel.

'Have you completed the Gemara on Yoma 38a?'

'Yes. I have.' Gabriel was smiling as he just completed the last sentence in the commentary when Rosh Yeshiva entered the room.

'What did you learn from there?'

'We live in the muted universe and are required to hear the song of the Angels. Not only are we asked to hear it, but have to understand its meaning, too. That song is only for us to hear, and what a disgrace if we cannot either hear or understand. Woe to us, if we cannot fulfil the will of our Creator!'

The Rosh Yeshiva looked at Gabriel with sapphire blue eyes sparkling with joy:

'There, you have the clarity now.'

Glossary

Aramaic - a language that originated among the Aramaeans in the ancient region of Syria, at the end of the 2nd millennium BCE, and later became one of the most prominent languages of the ancient Near East.

Asiyah - also known as Olam Asiyah, literally 'the World of Action' is the last of the four spiritual worlds of the Kabbalah — Atziluth, Beriah, Yetzirah, 'Asiyah — based on the passage in Isaiah 43:7.

Atziluth - known as the World of Emanations, or the World of Causes.

Au·to-da-fé – a noun meaning the burning of a heretic by the Spanish Inquisition.

Beriyah - literally 'the World of Creation', is the second of the four celestial worlds in the Tree of Life of the Kabbalah, intermediate between the World of Emanation (Atziluth) and the World of Formation (Yetzirah), the third world, that of the angels.

Bubby – (Yiddish) also bubbe–grandmother, granny

Elul - the sixth month in Jewish calendar

Gemara - rabbinical commentary on the Mishnah, forming the second part of the Talmud.

Genizah - is a storage area in a Jewish synagogue or cemetery designated for the temporary storage of worn-out Hebrew-language books and papers on religious topics prior to proper cemetery burial.

Ketoret - The incense offering in Judaism was related to offerings on the altar of incense in the time of the Tabernacle and the First and Second Temple period and was an important component of the liturgy in the Temple in Jerusalem.

Kibbutz - literally 'gathering, clustering' is a collective community in Israel that was traditionally based on agriculture. The first kibbutz, established in 1909, was Degania.

Kibbutznik - someone who lives and works on a kibbutz.

Khazars – were a semi-nomadic Turkic people with a confederation of Turkic-speaking tribes that in the late 6th century CE established a major commercial empire covering the southeastern section of modern European Russia, southern Ukraine, Crimea, and Kazakhstan. The Caspian Sea is still called the Khazar Sea.

Kuzari - The Kuzari, also known as the Book of the Kuzari, is one of the most famous works of the medieval Spanish Jewish philosopher and poet Judah Halevi, completed around 1140.

Marranos - (in medieval Spain) a Christianized Jew or Moor, especially one who merely professed conversion in order to avoid persecution.

Mishnah - an authoritative collection of exegetical material embodying the oral tradition of Jewish law and forming the first part of the Talmud.

Nu - (Yiddish) A multipurpose interjection meaning 'well?' 'so?', or 'so what?' in English.

Pogrom - an organized massacre of a particular ethnic group, in particular that of Jewish people in Russia or eastern Europe.

Rosh Hashana - the Jewish New Year, one of Judaism's holiest days. Meaning 'head of the year' the festival begins on the first day of the seventh month of the Hebrew calendar which falls during September or October.

Ruach HaKodesh – the Holy Spirit refers to the divine force, quality, and influence of God over the universe or over God's creatures.

Rosh Yeshiva - is the title given to the dean of a yeshiva, a Jewish educational institution that focuses on the study of traditional religious texts, primarily the Talmud and the Torah, and Jewish law.

Safta – grandmother in Hebrew

Shoah - the mass murder of Jewish people under the German Nazi regime during the period 1941-1945, the Holocaust.

Tzitzit – fringes on the corners of the garment worn by religious Jewish men.

Yetzirah - Yetzirah (also known as Olam Yetzirah) is the third of four worlds in the cabbalistic Tree of Life, following Atziluth and Beriyah and preceding Asiyah. It is known as the 'World of Formation'.

Zeidy – (Yiddish -zeyde) - grandfather

Printed in the United States
by Baker & Taylor Publisher Services